dream\drēm\: a strongly desired goal or purpose; something that fully satisfies a wish

Derek Redmond on the subject:

"A woman with a dream is dangerous—all that passion gives a man ideas. And *my* dream certainly isn't to become anyone's Mr. Right. You know where that will lead me—straight down the aisle to a woman in a white gown. But I don't have to worry about my confirmed bachelor status just yet. Because when a woman tries to bamboozle you (you didn't think Britt had me fooled for long, did you?), marriage isn't exactly the first thing on your mind...."

*Webster's Ninth New Collegiate
Dictionary, 1990

Dear Reader,

Ah, weddings… A blushing bride walks down the aisle toward Mr. Right, the guests' hearts burst with happiness, their eyes filled with tears of joy, their cameras poised for the big kiss. Until the bride passes one particular guest on her way. Suddenly, all eyes are on the groom's *recent* ex-fiancée, and whispers of "poor dear" can be heard above "The Wedding March."

Well, no one's going to call Emma Thorpe a "poor dear" in Christie Ridgway's wonderful novel, *The Wedding Date.* Invited to her ex-fiancé's wedding, Emma asks the most handsome stranger she can find to be her date. All the man needs to do is kiss her a few times, dance a few slow numbers—and fall in love with her by the cutting of the cake.

Britt Kingsley, in Janice Kaiser's terrific title *Just the Way You Are,* can't exactly expect to walk down the aisle anytime soon. Especially because the man she's in love with doesn't even know she exists. You see, before Britt ever realized he was Mr. Right material, she pretended to be someone else. And now he's fallen for the other woman—who's really her in disguise!

Next month, look for (extra-special!) Yours Truly titles by Marie Ferrarella and Lori Herter (see the sneak-preview blurbs in the back of this book)—two new novels about unexpectedly meeting, dating…and marrying Mr. Right!

Happy New Year!

Melissa Senate
Editor

Please address questions and book requests to:
Silhouette Reader Service
U.S.: 3010 Walden Ave., P.O. Box 1325, Buffalo, NY 14269
Canadian: P.O. Box 609, Fort Erie, Ont. L2A 5X3

JANICE KAISER

Just the Way You Are

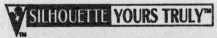

SILHOUETTE YOURS TRULY™

Published by Silhouette Books
America's Publisher of Contemporary Romance

SILHOUETTE BOOKS

ISBN 0-373-52011-5

JUST THE WAY YOU ARE

Copyright © 1996 by Belle Lettres, Inc.

Printed in U.S.A.

About the author

1984 was a landmark year for **JANICE KAISER.** She remarried, stopped practicing law and began her writing career. Since then, she has published nearly forty novels. In her spare time she has helped raise two stepchildren.

Janice is frequently asked if she misses practicing law. Her stock reply is that she's having far too much fun writing mysteries and romances, fantasy adventures and serious love stories to be bothered with real life.

For Jack and Susan Pfeiffer

Prologue

➤ ◄

Britt Kingsley stood in the tired old lobby of the Roxy Theater and stared out at Main Street. Her father, the Reverend Thomas Kingsley, was nearby, chatting with Norm Williams who'd buttonholed him just as they were about to leave. Both men were speaking earnestly about church business, but Britt wasn't paying close attention. Instead, she was thinking how strange it was to be back in Indiana, and how true the old saw was that you couldn't go home again.

Los Angeles seemed a million miles away. Still, if nothing else, the past few days had convinced her that L.A. was home now. Britt loved her father and appreciated the happy childhood he and her late mother had given her. Yet this visit had confirmed that win, lose or draw, her future lay elsewhere and there was no turning back.

After she'd fixed her father a big Caesar salad and seafood pasta to give him a taste of the California cuisine she'd come to love, she'd suggested they take in a movie. *Code Red,* a hot new thriller, was playing at the Roxy. On the plane coming from L.A. she'd read an article in *Variety* about the film and its director, Derek Redmond. It was a highly favorable piece, praising both. She'd told her father she just had to see it.

"I'm afraid all the shooting and explosions and car chases aren't my cup of tea, honey," he'd said. "Especially not during Christmas week. This is the time of year to see *It's A Wonderful Life*."

"I know that, Daddy, but it'll cost seven or eight bucks to see *Code Red* in Los Angeles and it's only four-fifty here. Can't pass up a bargain like that."

The Reverend Thomas Kingsley had tapped his daughter on the nose and jokingly said, "Another good reason to come home, Britt. Hays Crossing might be boring compared to California, but life's affordable here. And safe."

In the end, they'd compromised. He'd agreed to go with her to the movie theater—something he hadn't done in years—and she promised to rent *It's A Wonderful Life* and watch it with him on TV.

As Norm droned on, Britt wandered over to have a look at the latest movie posters. The tangy smell of buttered popcorn filled the air, evoking a thousand memories. She'd seen her first film ever at the Roxy. And this was where she and Tommy Bender had come for their first date in junior high. She didn't recall what film they'd seen, but they'd sat in the balcony and held hands the entire time.

That had been eleven or twelve years earlier, but in a way it seemed like forever. Yet the Roxy remained unchanged. The worn ruby red carpeting looked exactly the same as it had back then. Only the face of the kid behind the refreshment counter and the names of the films advertised on the posters were different.

Now that she thought about it, her father and Hays Crossing were sort of like the Roxy—they hadn't changed very much, either. The town had gotten a new Burger King. A farm-implements dealership had opened and a there was a new wing on the community hospital. Still, the essential nature of both her father and the town was the same. *She* was the one who was different.

Britt glanced back at her father, who was listening patiently to Norm's lament. She'd forgotten how trying a clergyman's life could be. Her mother had complained about that often while Britt was growing up, although she wouldn't have changed her husband for the world. Thomas Kingsley was a decent man, a man who gave unstintingly of himself whenever he was needed. That made being his child both easier and more difficult.

Britt wandered back to him. "Excuse me, Daddy," she said, touching his arm, "I'll wait out front while you finish your conversation. I want to get some air."

"Sorry to interrupt your evening, Britt," Norm Williams said.

"No problem, Norm," she told him. "I want to enjoy a little of this crisp Midwestern air."

"Guess it's a change from the palm trees and beaches out in California," he replied.

"True."

"Bet you don't miss having to shovel sidewalks, though."

"No, but I do miss the seasons," she said, turning for the door. "Finish your conversation."

"I'll be there in a few minutes," her father called after her.

Britt stepped onto the icy sidewalk that had been cleared of snow and sanded for better footing. The cold air stung her eyes. She turned up the collar of the bright pink parka she'd worn as a teenager and had left in the closet of her old room for just this sort of visit. Then she looked up and down the nearly deserted street. It was festooned with Christmas decorations and twinkling lights.

Main Street, like the old two-story brick house where she'd grown up, seemed smaller than she remembered. Smaller even than it had on her last trip back to Indiana. Its main appeal now, besides the comfort of familiarity, was that it was safe. L.A. was sparkling and glittery but it was a jungle, and living there was an adventure. Southern California was a place where people went to chase their dreams. That's why she'd gone there, and had been struggling so hard to make her dreams come true.

Britt stepped over to the glass case where the movie poster for *Code Red* was being displayed. How many times had she looked into that very case as a girl and imagined her own name and face on a poster for the world to see—her thick honey hair just brushing her shoulders, her firm jaw and the even features that the camera loved. A year and a half ago she had left Indiana with stars in her eyes, determined to make a name for herself as an actress, become famous.

Britt knew she was pretty by most standards, blond with the good looks of the girl next door. "Meg Ryanish" was the way her agent had billed her—girlish and womanly at the same time. And she was a good actress—not the most fabulous ever to hit Hollywood, but good enough to make it to the big screen. Talent was only the starting point, though. Everybody knew that. You needed luck and something else—a drive to succeed, a determination not to accept failure.

If there was an explanation for why she hadn't made it, that was it. She hadn't wanted it enough. She hadn't been willing to keep at it, no matter what. But she'd stuck it out for a year as she'd promised herself, getting a few bit parts along the way and a number of propositions having more to do with her sex appeal than her acting talent.

If her struggle had proved anything more than the fact that she wasn't meant to be an actress, it was that she had another love besides acting—a love that *was* powerful and consuming. She'd discovered it almost by accident. She had been reading a screenplay to prepare for an audition when she realized it wasn't well written. At least, not by her standards.

She had carefully analyzed the script, deciding she'd change the motivation here and the characterization there. Before she knew what was happening, she'd gotten out the old computer she'd used in college and started tinkering, and in the process had become a writer.

While she was in college her mother had died and left her a small inheritance, which she'd used to finance her trial year in Hollywood. There hadn't been enough money to stay there after she'd finally given up on an acting career, so she'd taken a job as a temp to pay the rent while she pounded away on her computer at night, churning out screenplays and honing her craft.

It was clear from the start that she'd discovered her life's work. She had a burning passion, an uncompromising determination to succeed—no matter the consequences. There had been no greater joy than the night she'd finished her first screenplay. It was at three o'clock in the morning on a balmy August night. She was alone in her apartment. In five hours she had to be at work, but she couldn't have felt more exhilarated. It had been a wonderful, miraculous moment.

Even though she hadn't been able to get an agent to take on that project, she had gotten some words of encouragement. Others recognized she had talent, and that was all she'd needed to keep her hooked. She wanted to see the world of her imagination come to life on the screen.

For the past few months she'd lived for that. And for the past few months she'd been learning how difficult it was to get a script read by someone who mattered. But she remained undaunted. By day she typed forms, answered phones and ran copy machines. At night she came alive, living in her imaginary world.

On Thanksgiving Day her father had phoned and invited her home for Christmas. She couldn't afford the price of a plane ticket, but promised that next year she'd find a way. A few days later a ticket arrived in the mail with a note from her dad, saying that both he and Hays Crossing deserved to see her. That made Britt realize she couldn't turn her back on the people she loved simply because she'd become obsessed.

Just then a flatbed truck piled high with bales of hay and carolers came up Main Street to the strains of "Jingle Bells." When it got opposite the Roxy, the truck stopped momentarily and the singers went into full voice, serenading her.

Britt recalled doing the very same thing not so many years before—riding through the streets of Hays Crossing, full of the holiday spirit, singing joyfully and having a good time. After thirty seconds, the truck moved on up the street. The carolers waved and Britt waved back, a sentimental tear coming to her eye. It wasn't the sort of thing one saw in L.A. It was no longer a part of her life, and she felt sad about that.

She watched the truck turn the corner and disappear from sight. For a moment or two she could hear the singing, but it soon grew faint and Main Street was quiet again.

The door opened behind her and her father stepped out onto the sidewalk. "Sorry, honey. Norm's been concerned about the shortfall in the budget and wanted to speak with me before the board meeting tomorrow night."

Thomas Kingsley was a slight man with refined features and an aesthetic, sensitive face. His once-sandy hair was now mostly white. He was quietly stately, a caring person. His greatest virtue as far as Britt was concerned, was that with her he could step out of the minister role and be a father first and foremost. She liked him as a person and considered him a friend.

"I understand," she said, taking his arm. "Don't forget, Daddy, I'm a veteran of lots of nights at home alone with Mama while you were attending meetings and calling on the sick or grieving."

They started up the sidewalk, headed for home. At Britt's insistence they'd walked the six blocks from the house to the movie theater.

"One of my biggest regrets is that I didn't fully appreciate how much I neglected you and your mother all those years," her father said.

"Don't be silly, Daddy. We knew you had important work to do. And we didn't consider ourselves neglected. Mama said she knew what she was getting into when she married a minister, and she never regretted it for one minute."

He patted her gloved hand. "You have the same generous spirit as your mother, sweetheart. I can't tell you how much I miss you both."

"Not being able to see you regularly is my only regret about leaving Indiana," she said.

"You really love it out there in California, don't you, honey?"

"I love writing. I can't tell you how much satisfaction it gives me. My regret is I'm not a bit more successful. But you know, the funny thing is that it doesn't matter. Not really. I'll keep on writing even if I never sell a screenplay."

"Strangely enough, I understand that. I feel the same way about my work."

"I'm a chip off the old block, I guess."

"The block you're a chip off is your mother, Britt. You're fortunate to be so much like her. I suppose that's why I feel so much more possessive of you than I should. It's also why I keep telling myself you have your own life to lead, and that I should be supportive but not domineering. But if I should slip now and then, I hope you'll understand."

Britt leaned over and kissed him on the cheek. "I couldn't ask for a better father."

He beamed happily.

They stopped at the corner and looked in the brightly lit window of Swig's Hobby and Toy Shop. It had been the origin of many of Britt's Christmas presents growing up. They watched the model train making its way around the snowy mountain.

"Funny how I never noticed that Santa always brought me the very thing that had delighted me most when you and Mama brought me down to Swig's to browse."

"We're all attached to our dreams, sweetheart, and none of us wants to let them go. Your mother and I always wanted to make your dreams come true when you were a child, and I want your dreams to come true now."

Britt wondered if he was making a subtle reference to her dream of being a screenwriter. "What are you trying to say, Dad? Tell me the truth. Do you think I'm chasing an empty dream by wanting to write?" she asked.

They waited for a car to turn the corner at Maple and then crossed the street, continuing on their way.

"I think you should do what makes you happy, Britt."

"Writing makes me happy. This isn't like when I wanted to act. I know it probably seems like it is to you, but it's not. This is . . . different. I feel it in my gut. And besides, I'm sure I have talent."

"You were a good actress, too, Britt. The trouble was, you picked a challenging and difficult field. It's shattered lots of hopes and dreams."

"I know you think I should pursue a more practical career, and you may be right, but this is something I just *have* to do. There's no other way to explain it."

"It's your life, honey, and you have to live it as you see fit. My only word of advice is to consider all your options, not just the work you do."

Britt knew he was referring to her personal life. One of his greatest concerns from the first had been about the people she would associate with in show business, especially the men. Her father had always had confidence in her judgment. He knew she was levelheaded. But his fear was that she wouldn't meet the sort of man she'd want to settle down with in a place like Hollywood.

She'd tried explaining that nice as many of the young men were in Hays Crossing, she simply didn't have anything in common with them—and never would. The men she'd met thus far in L.A. were a lot more interesting, but they had their limitations, too. And their dangers.

Her first morning home her father had mentioned that her high school boyfriend, Tim Ragsdale, had opened his own insurance agency and that he and his wife now had a second child. Britt's first reaction was that she was glad Tim had married Ellen Cross, not her. And yet, she liked Tim a lot. It was too bad she couldn't find someone with his character and decency, but who also shared her dreams.

The thought made her smile. Now *that* was a pipe dream if ever there was one.

They were soon beyond the business district. They walked past homes festooned with Christmas lights, painted wooden Santas on the roofs, snowmen on the lawns and glittering trees in the front windows. It was all so warm and familiar, and yet in an odd way vaguely sad. They both had been silent for a while.

"Tell me, Daddy, what did you think of *Code Red?*"

He thought for a moment, then replied, "I could have done with a little less shooting, but I was surprised how good it was, actually."

"That's because we cared about the characters and their problems. The most powerful drama is the human drama."

"Do you write that way, Britt?" her father asked.

"I try. I'm just a beginner, Daddy, but I'm learning."

"Well, tell me this. Was the script for *Code Red* significantly better than what you've done?"

"I'm sure it was, though I can't be objective about my own work. I'm determined to do something *as* good down the line, though. It may take a while, but I'll do it someday."

He patted her hand again. "I admire your spirit, honey."

They turned the corner and headed up their street. Britt squeezed her father's arm as the night chill started getting to her.

"The interesting thing about film is that it's a collaborative effort," she said. "The script is important, of course, but what the director and actors do with it is equally important. *Code Red* was brilliantly directed, in my opinion. He's awfully good."

"I didn't even notice who the director was."

"A man named Derek Redmond."

"Do you know him?"

Britt laughed. "Would that I did. He's one of the up-and-coming directors in Hollywood."

"Then he's young."

"I'd say early thirties."

"Believe me, Britt, from my perspective, that's young."

"*Code Red* was his first big commercial film. He's done a few smaller, low-budget flicks. This one put him on the map."

"Why don't you send him one of your screenplays?"

Britt sighed. "If only it was that easy. When you're a nobody, it's hard to get people to actually read anything you've written. In fact, it's hard to get a script into their hands in the first place. And even if you have an agent—which I don't—selling a script is tough. Only one out of a hundred screenplays ever gets made."

They'd come to her father's home and turned up the walk.

"And this is what you want to do as your life's work?" he asked.

She chuckled. "I know it sounds crazy, Daddy, but I'm determined. No matter what it takes, I'm going to find a way to make it as a writer. You'll see."

1

---➤◄---

Britt kept glancing at Harry Winslow's door, dreading the moment it would open. She didn't like going on job interviews any more than the next person, but that wasn't what was bothering her. This anxiety was different. Her moral integrity was on the line. She was about to do something she'd never thought she'd do—she was try to get a job under false pretenses.

The door opened and a short chubby man with thick glasses appeared. He looked to be in his early thirties and had an air of self-importance. Without even speaking to him, Britt decided he was bad news.

"Britt Kingsley?" he said.

Britt got to her feet and walked toward him. He checked her out in an obvious, unapologetic way, a smug grin on his face.

"I'm Harry Winslow," he said, offering her his hand. He was the personnel director of Continental Artists, the second-largest talent agency in Hollywood, and the man she had to get past in order to get the job.

"How do you do, Mr. Winslow?" she said, taking his clammy hand.

"I do fine," he said, twitching his brow provocatively. "Come right in."

Harry touched her waist as she passed by and Britt groaned inwardly. She hoped this wasn't going to be a casting-couch-type interview. Lord knew, she'd experienced more than her fair share of those. It had taken her a while, but she'd eventually learned that once she made up her mind not to be used that way, she could deal with the situation, though it had nearly always cost her the job. That had been okay when she'd been working as an actress, but getting on the inside of Continental Artists was essential to her plan—the plan to help promote her writing career.

Winslow gestured toward the visitor's chair, then took his place behind his desk. He folded his hands and leaned toward her, giving Britt a penetrating look, although the intimidating effect he evidently strived for was diminished somewhat by his weak chin.

"Look, Miss Kingsley," he said, "let me be blunt. There's a big red flag on your résumé from my standpoint. We might as well discuss it now, because there's no point continuing if we're not on the same page."

"What seems to be the problem, Mr. Winslow?"

"You're an actress and we can't have people working here with the intention of using the agency to further their acting career. C.A. has a firm policy against employees promoting their own interests with clients. Anybody caught doing it is summarily dismissed. No ifs, ands or buts about it."

"Mr. Winslow," she said firmly, "I am not an actress. I'm a *former* actress. There's a difference."

"How can I be sure what you say is true?"

"I don't know. I suppose you'll have to trust me." Even though that was true, Britt's words sent a stab of guilt through her.

Trust, honesty, integrity. Those had been the ideals she'd grown up with—the ones her parents had instilled in her. Britt wanted desperately not to lie. Yet she knew all too well that Hollywood was a place where fact and fiction often blurred. The town made its living on illusion. Everyone here tried their best to be what others wanted them to be. For a minister's kid from Indiana, squaring that with her core beliefs had not always been easy.

"A nice sentiment," Harry Winslow said, "but I'd rather make my decisions on the basis of cold, hard fact. When was the last time you read for a part?"

"It's been more than a year," she answered honestly. "As you can see from my résumé, I've been working as a temp with People Power for over a year now."

"Yes, but we all know that aspiring actors have to feed themselves. You could have squeezed in casting calls and small acting jobs."

"You could check with the Screen Actors Guild, Mr. Winslow."

"I will, but I thought I'd save myself the trouble if you had something you wanted to say." He grinned.

"You see, I've been down this road before. More than once."

"I admit I wanted to be an actress once, but that's behind me. I haven't read for any parts or registered with any talent agents since I signed as a temp. And in the two or three months before that, I scarcely left my apartment."

"Going through withdrawal, were you?"

"Yes," Britt replied. "That's exactly what it was."

Harry Winslow scrutinized her. Britt did her best to stare him down. So far, at least, every word she had uttered was true. What ate at her was what she wasn't saying—that she wanted so badly to become a successful writer that she would scheme and hustle and manipulate and do whatever it took to get her work in front of the people who counted.

The simple fact was, Continental Artists and agencies like it were essentially dating services for the movers and shakers in the film business. Anyone on the inside of a place like C.A. had access to those people. The trick would be figuring out how to promote herself without alienating the people who mattered. That wouldn't be easy, but she'd deal with it when the time came. For now, the problem was getting her foot in the door.

She'd tried everything she could think of to get her stuff read. Nothing had worked. Now she'd been reduced to trickery. Playing the Hollywood game—that's how she'd rationalized her scheme. It had helped some, to think of it in those terms, but not a lot.

There was one other factor in the equation, as well. Britt needed to survive, and Continental Artists was an excellent place to work. The pay was good and the people were interesting. Who wouldn't want to be in the same room with Keanu Reeves or Brad Pitt? Even if it was only to serve them coffee?

Britt had been fleshing out her plan with Allison O'Donnell, her good friend who lived in the apartment across the hall from her. "Think of it this way," Allison had said, "Even if you never get one of your screenplays sold, you'll still have to eat, buy shampoo and go to a movie now and then. You could work in worse places than C.A."

Britt had reluctantly embraced Allison's logic. But the one thing she hadn't done was call her father for advice. She didn't have to. She knew what he'd say.

Harry Winslow leaned back in his chair, clasping his hands behind his head. He was checking her out again, measuring her sex appeal, perhaps speculating on his chances with her. Not that big blue eyes and thick honey hair were all that unusual in Hollywood, but Britt could tell he fancied himself the Louis B. Mayer of personnel. She'd become an expert on spotting that sort of thing.

There were times when she lamented the fact that Hollywood was so image-oriented. Everybody had to look good. Style was everything and substance hardly mattered. She'd played the game. She wore her skirts short and got sixty-dollar haircuts when she could afford them, and sometimes when she couldn't. She flirted, too, because in L.A. people flirted as routinely as they chatted about the weather at home in Indiana.

"All right," Harry said after a few moments of reflection, "let's assume you've kicked the acting habit and gotten it out of your blood. Why do you want to work for C.A.? Do you expect to get some kind of vicarious pleasure from being around people who have made it?"

Britt drew a long breath. "I'm looking for a position with career possibilities and I just didn't have that at People Power. I see that sort of opportunity here." She looked him in the eye, but that didn't prevent another pang of conscience.

"Why a talent agency? There are careers to be had in law firms, brokerage houses, whatever."

Britt shifted uncomfortably, recrossing her legs. Harry watched her every move, probably thinking he'd backed her into a corner. Britt knew she had to play this very carefully.

"Having been an actress briefly, I know the business," she said. "I can't say that about law or investments. It seems to me I'd be more effective working in a field in which I've had at least some experience."

Harry Winslow leaned back in his chair, rubbing his chin. He did his best to look unconvinced. "Let's say I'm your best friend. Tell me about your goals. Assuming we hire you, where do you see yourself in five years?"

"Occupying one of those offices out there. I see my-self making people stars and contributing to their success."

"You want to be an agent."

"Yes," she said, elevating her chin to signal determination. Britt was acting now. "I don't want to be a secretary forever," she went on. "I'm willing do a damned fine job of it for however long it takes to learn the business. I know I've got to pay my dues. But sooner or later I'll be ready for more."

The skepticism on his face had been transformed into glowing pride. Britt sensed that she'd convinced him. He'd decided she was all right, perhaps even an unpolished gem. That, after all, was his mission in life. She could almost hear him gloating to his associates. "I've found a real firecracker. Dedication, ambition, drive, T&A—a girl that's got it all."

"Very impressive," he said aloud. "You sounded like you meant that. Couldn't be you gave up on your acting career too quickly, could it?" He gave her a wink.

Britt wanted to slug him, but she kept her poise, knowing he was baiting her. "I'm a hard worker," she said simply. "All my references will vouch for that."

"They already have," he replied, grinning smugly. "You check out. I just had that question about your real motives. I had to satisfy myself you were on the up and up." He let his eyes roll down her, signaling his satisfaction.

Britt's first reaction was to ask him to get on with it, but she told herself that she had to let him do his thing.

Once she was hired, Harry Winslow wouldn't matter. But right now he still stood between her and access to some of the leading producers and directors in Hollywood.

Harry suddenly swung his chair around and stared out the window at the smog. All Britt could see over the back of the chair was the top of his head with its tangerine-size bald spot. "Tell you what I'm going to do," he said. "I'm going to send you down to Miranda Maxwell. The position we've been talking about reports to her. Miranda's our newest partner, a real gogetter. She's asked for someone with initiative, a fast learner. This is your chance to prove yourself to her. What happens from here on out is up to you." He turned his chair back around to face her. He was steepling his fingers. "Remember, at C.A. we view former actresses with skepticism. Don't think this is the way to the silver screen, because it isn't."

"No, I understand."

He reached for the phone, letting his eyes flicker over her. "I'll let Miranda know you're on the way down."

"So, Britt, did you have a nice little chat with our Mr. Winslow?"

Miranda Maxwell was thirty-five, English, darkly attractive with pale, pale skin, smooth as porcelain—the sort that was as common in the British Isles as raindrops. Britt's Grandmother Kingsley, who'd been born in Wales, had told her that.

"He's ... unusual," Britt said in response to Miranda's question.

"Good job, you're a diplomat. Heaven knows, it doesn't hurt in this line of work," Miranda Maxwell said. "Don't repeat this, but Harry's our stalking horse. If an applicant survives half an hour with him, we know she's got grit. From this point forward it's qualifications and chemistry." Miranda looked down at the résumé on her desk and contemplated it for a moment.

Britt felt better already. It was nice to know Miranda had a sense of humor, and a sense of proportion. Harry Winslow had made her wonder if coming to work at C.A. would be such a good idea, after all.

The real problem—the dilemma that wouldn't seem to go away—was that to get the job she had to keep her true agenda hidden. Her determination to succeed as a writer at all costs was so fierce that she was no longer sure in her heart what was right and what was wrong. The desperation that had been building over the past several months had blurred everything.

It was October now. Another year had passed. She had six screenplays in her drawer and not a single offer to show for all her effort. If she'd learned anything this past year, it was that nobody in Hollywood gave you something for nothing. You had to fight for every break, every opportunity. But did it mean she had the moral right to engineer her own breaks? That was the question.

While Miranda Maxwell studied her application, Britt checked out the office. It had a certain panache even though it was not very large. The decor was eclectic. There were several framed prints, mostly nineteenth-century theater scenes. A fine antique mahogany desk. Lots of books. And photos of family and celebrities. Miranda in evening clothes with Sir John Gielgud and Sir Anthony Hopkins. Miranda, looking much younger, with Vanessa Redgrave. Miranda in the fatherly embrace of Sir Richard Attenborough. Miranda standing between Kenneth Branagh and Emma Thompson, everyone smiling, especially Miranda.

Britt wanted to ask if she really knew all those people, or if she just happened to get photographed with them. Miranda was either well connected, or she had a knack for getting invited to parties. A bouquet of mixed flowers sat on the corner of the desk. Britt savored the perfume of it.

"No doubt Harry gave you his speech about forswearing screen and stage to work here," Miranda said, looking up.

"Yes."

Miranda studied her. "You've got the looks and a definite presence. What kept you from making it?"

"I guess I didn't have the burning desire. Not deep down."

"That usually is key. Some are luckier than others, but in this business a determination to succeed is essential."

Britt nodded, knowing that Miranda was describing her as a screenwriter, not an actress.

"No regrets?" Miranda asked.

Britt knew that although more subtle, Miranda was asking the same question Harry Winslow had. "My acting phase is over," she said.

"I don't mind a person 'having done,'" Miranda said. "To be truthful, I consider it an advantage. Always helps to know what it's like to be on the other side."

Britt nodded, pleased that her past didn't constitute a black mark. Of course, that still left the problem of her present ambitions.

"All the same," Miranda went on, "I can't have staff mucking with my clients. There'll be no self-promotion. When a star or director is with their agent, it's like visiting Mother. This environment must be safe, supportive and salubrious. The three *S*s, I call them. We're looking out for *them,* not for ourselves."

The admonition made Britt feel sick. Promoting herself was *exactly* what she had in mind and Miranda had put the moral issue squarely on her shoulders. What should she do? Her mind raced. She could say she'd changed her mind and walk out. But then she would be without a job—and she did need to eat. Perhaps there was a way she could be honest with Miranda and still take the position. After all, fledgling screenwriters needed daytime work, too.

"I trust you can live with that," Miranda said.

"Yes, Miss Maxwell."

"Miranda, by all means. Good heavens." She smiled faintly. "I only *look* this old," she said, making Britt laugh. Miranda glanced at the résumé again. "And you are...twenty-six, I see. Just the right age for a younger sister.''

Britt smiled, liking the woman, although in a way that only made things worse.

Miranda placed a well-manicured finger against her cheek, assessing her. She was in a plain white blouse and dark wool skirt. Understated earrings. Thin gold watch. No rings. Safe, supportive, salubrious. The words went through Britt's head.

''Tell me about yourself, love,'' Miranda said. ''It's a ruddy bore, I know, but we are our pasts, aren't we?''

Britt shifted uneasily. She felt like such a phony. ''Well, let's see...''

''You can skip the parts the law won't allow me to question,'' Miranda said. ''Your rules about employment in this country are too bloody confusing for me to keep straight.''

Britt smiled. ''I don't have any dark secrets in my past. I grew up in Indiana. Majored in theatrical arts at the University of Michigan. After graduation I returned to my hometown and took a job in the local recreation department, teaching theater arts to children. Then I did a stint in regional theater, doing some acting, but mostly behind-the-scenes work. Everything from scenery, props and lighting to typing letters and reading scripts.

''Finally, I decided if I was ever going to get anywhere I'd have to head for L.A. So I came here a couple of years ago with stars in my eyes.''

"I know the story well," Miranda said. "But now your dream is to be an agent. Harry's made a note to that effect."

Britt was sorry now she'd come up with that story, but if she hadn't said something when Harry had pressed her, she'd have found herself in the parking lot five minutes later, headed for her next job interview. "I admit to being ambitious," she said, waffling.

"Enough about that," Miranda replied. "Let's discuss this position. I should tell you how I work and how you'll be expected to fit in. No point in going on if it doesn't appeal to you."

Miranda gave her a rundown of her client list, discussing the way she liked to work. She also spoke of the individuality of each of her clients.

Fifteen minutes of rapport-building passed before Miranda leaned back in her chair and said, "I've got a good feeling about you, Britt. I think we'd make a good team. I want you to be my administrative assistant."

Britt was elated. The door had finally opened. She'd be on the inside! It might take weeks or months, but sooner or later she'd find a chance to talk to someone about her screenplays—someone who might help her get her work read...or optioned...or, please God, produced.

The hell of it was, in order to do that she'd have to live a lie. She'd done her best to rationalize that, though. She had no intention of hurting anyone and until the time came when she did have a chance to put her work in the hands of someone who might appreciate it, she'd work her tail off, do the job to the best of her ability.

"Well, ducks," Miranda said, "what do you say?"

Britt had to pull herself together. "I'm speechless," she finally managed. "But I couldn't be happier."

"Super!" Miranda Maxwell seemed genuinely pleased. "I'm sure we'll get on fabulously. I must warn you, though, there's loads of work. In a week I'm off to London for a fortnight, so I'm glad to see you can start immediately. It's essential I have you in place and trained in the basics before I'm off. I'm not keen on going just now, but it can't be helped. Family business. But never mind, we'll be talking daily while I'm gone. You'll be my lifeline to my clients, Britt, so you'll have to be up to speed, as we say."

"I'll certainly do my best."

Miranda beamed. "The hectic pace of life at C.A. can be a bloody nuisance, but of course I wouldn't trade it for anything. Let's hope you feel the same."

"I'm sure I will, Miss Maxwell—Miranda, I mean."

Miranda picked up the phone. "I'll just give Harry a ring and tell him to start the paperwork on you." She spoke briefly, saying that Britt would be down to see him presently, then put down the phone and sighed. "That's done, though I'm afraid you'll have to humor Harry a bit more. Forms, you know."

Britt nodded. She looked at Miranda and had a tremendous urge to blurt out the truth, to tell her that she was really an aspiring screenwriter, a woman who des-

perately wanted to get her work into the hands of the
right people.

"What is it, dear?" Miranda asked, fingering her
necklace. "You look distraught. Surely the prospect of
seeing Harry's not that horrific."

"No, I'm just letting it all sink in."

Miranda nodded and got to her feet. So did Britt.
Then Miranda came around her desk and shook Britt's
hand. "Off you go. Half an hour or so with Harry and
you're free till tomorrow at eight-thirty, sharp. Come
prepared, ducks. Before I leave for London, you're going to know my clients as well as I!"

2

"So, a week on the job and already you're in charge." Sally Farland was at the door, cheerful and pleasantly plump in another of her short leather skirts and boots. She grinned as she peered into Britt's office.

"In charge of answering the phone and relaying messages to London," Britt said. "I haven't had to make any earthshaking decisions so far."

"Never fear, Miranda will keep you hopping," Sally said. She touched her unruly brown curls. "She's ambitious, that one. Smart lady. And a good boss."

Sally was Gordon Mallik's assistant. Gordon, an affable, balding man of forty-five with apple cheeks, had several actor clients, including two or three of Hollywood's biggest names. During Britt's third day on the job, Carrie Hunter had visited him.

Britt couldn't help staring when the actress had passed her in the hall. Since her Oscar nomination, Carrie Hunter was one of the hottest names in the business. She'd dropped by to talk scripts with Gordon as Sally had run around frantically, bringing them Evian water, or getting somebody or other on the phone. The energy level in the place always went up, Britt discovered, when a big star was visiting.

Work at C.A. was stimulating, and Miranda's list of director clients looked absolutely mouthwatering to a budding screenwriter. The biggest name among her clients was Oliver Wheatley. He'd had one Oscar nomination and was a contender for a second. Like many of Miranda's clients, he was British. Miranda had explained that her goal now was to increase the number of Americans on her list. She'd been working hard to cultivate the younger, up-and-coming American directors. "Get them early," she'd told Britt. "That's my philosophy."

Britt gave Sally a woebegone look. "A week isn't much preparation time to be left alone. I hope I'm ready for this."

"You'll be fine. Gordon and I will help if you need anything. He promised Miranda he'd watch over you."

"She didn't seem too concerned when she left. But there's so much to remember—who I can say what to, and what not to say to certain people. There are the ones to be businesslike with, and the ones to kiss and hug."

"Fear not. My extension is your panic button," Sally assured.

Sally had been helpful from day one. They'd gone to lunch twice and Sally hadn't been shy about giving her the skinny on the office, from the "working slob's perspective," as she called it.

"I'll do my best," Britt said.

"Piece of cake," Sally said, giving her a thumbs-up. "Got to get back to my desk. By the end of the week you'll be loving it. Trust me."

Alone at her desk, Britt checked her list of things to do. Miranda wanted her to call Ian Harbury's L.A. publicist and reiterate that under no circumstances could Westley Asquith agree to an interview with Joyce Wilson. According to Miranda, Joyce had tried to crucify Oliver Wheatley in a recent interview.

"Joyce Wilson may still be fighting the Revolutionary War, as you call it," Miranda had explained, "but my clients are not, and I won't have them treated in such a shoddy manner. Westley simply can't be allowed to speak with the woman."

Britt couldn't make the call until midafternoon. Nothing else had to be done just then so she pulled out the client list, comparing the names with her notes. Miranda had discussed some of the clients' career goals with her, but the thing Britt cared about most—which of them might be interested in her own work—was not something she could easily bring up without raising suspicion. And besides, except for Oliver Wheatley, Britt didn't know enough about any of them to judge whether or not they were likely to be interested in one of her scripts. She'd have to bide her time and watch for an opportunity.

The phone rang and Britt jumped to answer it. It was Tiffany, the receptionist. "Britt, Derek Redmond is on line three for Miranda."

Britt's mouth dropped open. Derek Redmond! Ever since she'd seen *Code Red* with her father the previous December she'd been fascinated by the director and his work. His next film was due to be released by TriStar soon and she couldn't wait to see it. In fact, Derek Redmond had been on her mind a great deal during the past ten months.

It seemed pieces on him kept turning up in newspapers and periodicals. At the dentist's office she'd picked up a copy of *People* Magazine only to find a picture of him and a short article. And then a few months later there was a blurb on him in Walter Scott's "Personality Parade" column in *Parade*. A reader had asked for particulars on his personal life. Scott had said Redmond led a very private life, avoiding the Hollywood social whirl. There was no particular lady in his life, although he'd been seen in public with several different young women, none of them celebrities. Scott had used the word "charismatic" to describe Derek Redmond, which fit perfectly with Britt's perception of him. Ever since seeing *Code Red* she'd had a crush on him.

He was the first director to whom she'd sent the script of her thriller, *Flash Point*. She'd been certain he would love it, but the envelope had been returned unopened with a note saying that he didn't read unsolicited manuscripts except when sent through agents.

Now Derek Redmond was on the telephone, waiting to speak with her! She couldn't believe it.

"Tiffany..." Britt said, feeling a sudden panic.

"Yes?"

"Did you tell him Miranda's in London?"

"No, I didn't say a thing, except that I'd put him through to her office. You'll have to tell him whatever she wants. Got to go, kid. Got another call."

Britt looked at the flashing light on her console. Her hand shaking, she picked up the receiver. "Miranda Maxwell's office," she croaked, her insides quavering.

"Hi, this is Derek Redmond," he said easily. "Is Miranda in, please?"

"No...no, I'm sorry she isn't, Mr. Redmond. She won't be back for...at least...uh—"

"Well, I don't actually need to talk to her. Are you her assistant?"

"Yes, sir."

"I'll bet you have a name," he gently chided.

"Yes, it's Britt," she replied.

"Britt, huh? But you aren't a Brit yourself by the sound of your voice."

"No, sir."

He chuckled. "Well, it wasn't very funny, was it? Not even a very good pun. Sorry."

It was only then that she realized he was trying to be humorous. She flushed, not knowing what to say.

"Maybe you could give Miranda a message for me, Britt," he said.

"Certainly."

"Last week I did breakfast with Oliver Wheatley. We were comparing notes on the business and I told him the hardest part was finding a good script. I really admired *Go Fish*. It wasn't hackneyed. When I asked Oliver how he found the script, he said Miranda had put him onto it. Claimed she had a wonderful eye, a real sense for the director's artistic impulses.

"Which is the long way of saying that I wanted to know if Miranda's seen anything that might be good for me. Ask her to give it some thought, if you would, then maybe she and I could talk."

"Yes, I will, Mr. Redmond." Britt's brain was reeling. Dear God, was this the opportunity she'd been waiting for? If so, she had to say something. Fast. *Carpe diem.* Seize the moment. "Uh... I'm sure Miranda will want to know what it is you're looking for, exactly."

"That's the problem. I'm not sure. Not another thriller, I don't want to get typecast. That happens with a short résumé, I know, and if I want to be regarded as diverse, I might as well start branching out now. From what Oliver said, Miranda's perfectly in tune with that."

"I'm sure she is. I know she's a fan of yours."

"Oh, really?"

"Yes. We were talking about *Code Red* the other day. Miranda thinks you have a lively, fresh style. In my opinion, *Code Red* was everything a good thriller should be. It had heart as well as thrills."

"What a nice compliment, Britt. Thank you. I'd like to take full credit for the success of the film, but I was working with a good screenwriter and some very talented actors. It's nice to know that people appreciate the things you strive to accomplish, though."

"You have millions of fans, I'm sure."

"You seem to be knowledgeable about filmmaking," he said.

"I try to keep up."

"Miranda's fortunate to have you working for her."

"Thank you."

She felt equal measures of elation and terror. Derek Redmond sounded like a nice person, somebody she could talk to about the things she cared about. The fantasy image of him in her mind was apparently more accurate than she could possibly have imagined.

"I've got to run, Britt," he said. "It's been very nice talking to you. Have Miranda give me a buzz, will you? Let me give you my number."

Britt jotted it down, her heart pounding like crazy. For a solid year she'd been reduced to considering ploys like throwing a brick with a script tied to it over some producer's garden wall or lying down in front of a director's limo—anything to put her work into the hands of somebody who mattered. And now, who was at her fingertips but Derek Redmond! Fate had to have done this for a reason.

"Mr. Redmond," she said quickly before he could hang up, "have you given much thought to romantic comedy?"

There was a short pause. "What do you mean? Nora Ephrom-type stuff?"

"Yeah, but maybe a little more down-home. Not so New York."

There was a hesitation on the line. Britt felt her stomach knot.

"Why?" he asked. "Does Miranda have something along those lines she's shopping for?"

Britt swallowed hard. "Well...I heard her talking about a script the other day, saying it had tremendous possibilities, but that it needed the right director."

"Hmm," Derek said. "Who's the writer?"

Panic seized her. "Oh, an unknown. Miranda came across it purely by chance." Britt felt her cheeks burn. She closed her eyes and the sexy photo of Derek Redmond in *People* came to mind.

"Does the screenplay have a title?" he asked.

She bit her lip, hesitating. Then she plunged ahead and said, *"Dream Girl."*

"Hmm. Well, you've piqued my curiosity, Britt. Never can tell what gem might by lying around waiting to be snatched up, can you?"

"No, that's certainly true." She almost forgot to breathe.

"Listen," he said, "tell Miranda I'd be interested in seeing *Dream Girl.* Maybe when she calls we can discuss it."

Britt was so excited, she thought she'd expire on the spot. "I'll tell her, Mr. Redmond."

"Great. I'll be looking forward to her call."

Redmond said goodbye but it took Britt a few seconds after he'd hung up for her to have the presence of mind to put down the phone. What had she done? How on earth could she have Miranda call Derek Redmond from London and talk about a script she knew nothing about? Dare she tell her boss the truth? No, to Miranda it would look like she was feathering her own nest—which she was. Even if Britt's script was the best she'd read in ten years, Miranda would be furious.

Britt stared at the number Derek Redmond had given her. Maybe she could call him back and say she'd been mistaken. On the other hand, what if she sent her script over to him and he loved it? What if he actually wanted to do it?

If that happened, she wouldn't need this job. On second thought, maybe she would. Even if he optioned *Dream Girl,* it did not guarantee that the film would get produced—and that was when the writer made serious money; when the movie was actually shot.

Britt put her fingers to her fiery cheeks. This was insane. Absolutely crazy. Yet she was sure it was the golden opportunity she'd been waiting for. This was her chance to put her script in the hands of a director with a guarantee that it would be given serious attention.

But the fly in the ointment was that he wanted to talk to Miranda. How could she handle that? Send the script over with a cheery note saying that Miranda was headed for London and would chat with him when she returned? If he decided to phone her in England, the jig would be up. No, she had to figure out something else. But what?

Britt looked at her telephone for the millionth time in less than an hour. Never had she felt so torn. In fact, she couldn't remember ever feeling this indecisive. It had been awfully hard telling her father she'd decided to move to L.A., but that wasn't because she was unsure about what she wanted to do—it was because she loved him and knew he'd be disappointed. This was a horrible quandary. A voice in the back of her mind kept saying, "Pick up the phone, do it!" But still she hesitated.

Her basic plan was good—if she could pull it off. The problem was she hadn't practiced the accent. Still, she'd been around Miranda long enough to know how she talked, and she had a darned good ear. Her drama teachers had agreed that her accents were her greatest talent. In class skits she'd done Edith Bunker, both Scarlett O'Hara and Prissy from *Gone With the Wind*, and even Marlon Brando as the Godfather. The real question now was whether she'd be able to do a serious businesswoman talking about serious business. And even if she could, did she dare?

She wrung her hands, torn, uncertain, sure one moment that her whole life had been leading up to this point, positive the next that God would strike her dead for her perfidy and deceit. She told herself that this was why she'd come to work for C.A. It was all part of the plan. But now that the moment of truth had come, instead of rushing ahead she was asking herself how anything so necessary could be wrong. Surely courage would be rewarded. Fear and guilt could only lead to defeat.

Finally, riding the crest of a wave of fierce determination, she stepped into Miranda's office and closed the door. When she shut her eyes Britt could hear Miranda's voice, her crisp British middle-class accent. Educated, but not too educated. Sophisticated, but not too sophisticated.

"You'll love it here, ducks," she intoned, testing her voice. "But you'll earn every penny, I promise you that. No rest for the wicked." Britt had to laugh. How prophetic *that* remark had been.

She sat down in Miranda's chair, took a deep breath, and dialed the number Derek Redmond had given her. He answered himself.

"Derek," she said in her best BBC voice, "this is Miranda Maxwell over at C.A. My young lady tells me you rang me this morning."

"Yes, Miranda, thanks for calling back. I'm sure Britt told you I was looking for a special script, something fresh, and that she'd brought *Dream Girl* to my attention. I'm intrigued by the notion of a romantic comedy. So the question is, can I entice you to let me have a peek?"

"Oh, my."

"Is something wrong?"

"Derek, dear, you aren't supposed to know about that script. It's not something I'm officially representing, which means it doesn't exist." She paused a heartbeat. "I'll have to talk to Britt about her loose lips."

"You mean it's unavailable?"

"Well, I didn't exactly say that, now, did I? You see, I always have something interesting in hand, love, but I try to direct the best projects toward my clients. You understand, surely."

"Well, certainly. But Britt made it sound like this might not be appropriate for your regular clients."

"She did, did she?" Britt's Miranda showed a touch of indignation.

"I might have made some unwarranted assumptions," he quickly said. "Don't blame her. In fact, I kind of forced her to tell me what she knew. She was doing her best to look out for your interests, Miranda, believe me."

Britt put her hand over the mouthpiece. She couldn't help a little giggle. He was being sweet, protecting her from Miranda's wrath. What a decent thing to do. It was endearing and made her heart reach out to him. "This is Hollywood," she said, pulling herself together and getting back in character. "Which means we're all selling something, aren't we, love?"

"Thanks for being understanding."

"Continental Artists is in business to serve, Derek."

"Would you tell me a little about *Dream Girl?*" he asked.

"There's no harm in that, I should think. Well, let's see.... Innocent but clever country girl—say, Winona Ryder—meets hip young man from the city—say, Brad Pitt—and they have a romance. Gordon described it as a Generation X *Bridges of Madison County.*"

"I get the picture. I want to see it."

"Hmm. You've put me on the spot now, haven't you?"

"If I'm out of line, just say so," he said.

Britt felt a rush of power—power as she'd never known it before. Here she was, with one of the brightest young directors in Hollywood practically begging her to send him her script. But then she realized that her power was false. The instant she was discovered, she'd go down like the *Hindenburg*.

"Are you quite sure you want to see it, Derek? It's good, but it has absolutely nothing in common with *Code Red*."

"That's exactly what I want, Miranda. Something completely different."

"I see." Britt allowed a pregnant pause, almost bursting with excitement. She was on a roll, but on terribly thin ice. She couldn't lose sight of that.

"You didn't have somebody else in mind for it, did you?" Derek asked.

"No, love. I don't officially have control of the project, but of course that's a technicality. I could have a word with the writer and fix things up in the blink of an eye, but..."

"But what?"

Britt didn't know where her words were coming from. It was almost as though she was sitting at her computer and the dialogue was spilling out. "Well, to be bloody frank about it," she said with uncanny assurance, "an associate of mine promised Ron Howard a look, or at least I think he did. Gordon was the one who first brought the script to my attention, you see."

"When will you know?"

"If you're that eager, I suppose I could give him a tinkle now. Do you prefer to hold or should I ring you back?"

"I'll hold."

Britt pushed the Hold button and all but bounced in her chair. "Bloody hell!" she said excitedly. "Miranda couldn't have done better herself." She spun the chair around, whooping with laughter. "What do you think, Gordon, love? Shall we let the poor sod have a wee peek at Britt Kingsley's masterpiece?"

She stared at the flashing light, hoping Derek Redmond's heart was pounding as furiously as hers. God, she wished she could see his face.

And then a curious feeling came over her. In the midst of her excitement she thought of his kindness, his consideration. They'd only had a couple of conversations, yet she was beginning to get a strong sense of him. And what she'd seen, she liked.

But was that good? After all, it wasn't a relationship she was striving for—not a personal relationship, anyway. This was business. She had to think of Derek Redmond as a professional opportunity.

Britt turned her attention to the phone. She stared at the flashing light, counted to twelve, then pushed the button. "You may have it, if you wish, Derek," she announced airily. "But only for a few days. Will that do?"

"Fine. Courier it to me?"

"Tomorrow."

"Sold," he said.

"You're an easy man to deal with, Derek Redmond."

"However this turns out, Miranda, we'll do lunch soon."

"That would be lovely, but I'm booked for London in a few days' time. We might have to do it later."

"I never forget a kindness," Derek said. "Oliver told me you walked on water, and now I believe it."

"You aren't sweet-talking me, are you, dear boy?"

"Yes."

"I admire your candor," she said.

"And I like your style, Miranda. We'll have to talk about the future, regardless how things turn out with *Dream Girl*."

"Delighted, of course."

"I look forward to getting the script. *Ciao.*"

Britt let the receiver fall gently into the cradle, then leaned back heavily in Miranda's chair. The sober reality of it all hit her like the proverbial ton of bricks. "Dear God," she murmured, "what have I done?"

3

———◄—

Britt lived on the third floor of a fifty-year-old apartment building in West Hollywood, off Sunset Boulevard. She parked her ancient Toyota up the street from it and walked back toward her complex, her mind going a mile a minute. Derek Redmond actually wanted to see *Dream Girl!* In fact, he'd practically *begged* to read it!

This was a red-letter day. Yet with her euphoria was a nagging sense of guilt she couldn't shake off. All afternoon she'd struggled to rationalize her duplicity, telling herself that in Hollywood, *everyone* was on the make; everyone hustled everyone else. True, once you had fame and status, you played the game with less desperation, but you still played it. Self-promotion was what Hollywood was all about. But no matter how hard Britt tried to convince herself that was the way the business worked, she still felt uneasy.

Arriving at the entrance to her building, she opened her mailbox and removed a utility bill, a credit-card statement and some advertising flyers. The problem was, she was a minister's daughter at heart and her conscience simply wouldn't let her enjoy her triumph.

Annoyed with herself, Britt started trudging up the stairs. The stairwell had a distinctive musty smell, overlaid with the scent of cleaning solvent. For some reason it triggered a rare sensation of homesickness—recollections of her parents' home. She could almost see herself sitting in her father's study when she was nine, listening to the regulator clock ticking as he read the letter from her teacher saying that she'd allowed a classmate to copy her homework assignments. Thomas Kingsley had mournfully removed his reading glasses, then asked what had happened. She'd only gotten half a sentence out before bursting into tears.

It wasn't only the shame, it was the mortification of having let her father down, of having failed in his eyes. To this day, his words rang in her ears. "Good intentions aren't all that matter, Britt. It's whether what you do is right. First, to thine own self be true. Remember that. You'll never be sorry."

So what did the moral principle she'd learned that autumn day in Indiana so long ago tell her about the way to deal with Derek Redmond now? Did she call him up and confess that it was all a hoax? Should she try to explain that she really wanted to succeed because of the merit of her work, not because of a phony story or false endorsement? Did she tell him she was a wannabe like hundreds of others, scratching and clawing to get their work read at any cost? Should she suggest he ought to read her screenplay anyway? Fat chance. He'd laugh in her face.

Britt had climbed to the third-floor landing when the door to Allison O'Donnell's apartment opened. Her friend, who worked as a property manager at Paramount, smiled at her.

"Hi, kiddo," Allison said cheerfully. "Discover any new stars today?"

"Yeah, one."

"Good for you! Keep it up and you'll be a partner before your boss gets back from England."

"Dream on, Allison," Britt said as she fumbled in her purse for her key. "I'll be happy if I still have a job when Miranda gets back."

"Don't despair. The first month on a new job is always stressful," Allison said. "But I sympathize. I really do." She put her hand on Britt's arm.

Allison was tall, lean and gangly—not homely, but not pretty. She had a long narrow face and big brown eyes behind her glasses. Her thick, dark brown hair was her best feature. Britt liked her because she was always upbeat. Allison was also kind and generous, a great person to have as a friend.

"I was just on my way down to the supermarket," Allison said. "Anything I can get for you while I'm there?"

"Yeah, a bottle of cyanide—or truth serum—whichever's on sale." Britt put her key in the lock and turned the dead bolt.

"Hey, Britt, what's wrong? I thought you were sort of down at first, but you sound really upset."

She turned to face her friend. "Why should I be upset? Derek Redmond asked to see my script today. He's all excited about it."

Allison blinked. "So what's the problem?"

Britt groaned and rolled her eyes. "You'd never believe me, if I told you."

"Maybe you should tell me anyway," Allison replied, her tone growing more serious. "Shall I invite myself in, or are you going to?"

"I thought you were headed for the store."

"That can wait. I don't want to return and find the paramedics carrying you out of here on a stretcher."

Britt gestured for Allison to come in. The apartment was a tiny one-bedroom, furnished mostly with rented pieces. Britt had hoped to replace the rental stuff with things of her own, but she hadn't worked steadily enough to be able to afford much.

Her most valuable possession was her computer. It sat on the small desk against one wall. The decor consisted mostly of movie posters, candles, dried flowers and her books. She'd always been a reader and had dragged her collection around everywhere, putting her beloved books on shelves made with bricks and boards covered with contact paper. The life of an aspiring writer was not much different from that of a student. Sometimes Britt felt as though she hadn't grown up.

"I'm sure I'm blowing things out of proportion," she said. "I guess it's guilt." She tossed her purse on a chair and headed for the kitchen.

"Guilt?" Allison followed her to the kitchen and stood at the door.

"How about a glass of wine?" Britt asked, taking two glasses down from the cupboard and getting the jug of white wine from the refrigerator.

"Sounds like it might be a good idea."

They sat at the tiny kitchen table as Britt began relating what had happened that day. After she'd finished telling the story, Allison leaned back in her chair, pondering her.

"I don't see why you're so down in the dumps. I think what you did is clever." She beamed. "A damned good marketing ploy. It's even sort of funny."

"At the time I was halfway pleased with myself, I admit, though the other half of me was scared to death." Britt took a slug of wine. "But now that I'm able to get a little perspective on what I've done, I can see how dishonest it was."

"Maybe you're having second thoughts because you're afraid."

"Afraid of what?"

"Failure. You're afraid Derek Redmond won't like your screenplay."

"Allison, that's ridiculous. I want him to read *Dream Girl* more than anything."

"Really? Are you sure that deep down the thought of rejection doesn't terrify you?"

"Of course, I'm nervous. But I want my screenplay read. Look at the lengths I've gone to."

"Then why are you having second thoughts?"

Britt grimaced. "Well, I don't like the fact that I've had to lie and cheat to set things up."

"And so you're thinking of not sending the script."

"Well..." Britt agonized. "Do *you* think I should send it?"

"Of course I do."

"Why?"

"Come on, Britt, let's be honest," Allison said. "All any director cares about is getting good material. What does it really matter how it gets into his hands? You found a clever gimmick to promote yourself, that's all. In my opinion, you should be congratulated for your ingenuity."

Allison's words of reassurance made her feel better. The cloud that had been slowly gathering all day seemed momentarily to lift. "I suppose if nobody's hurt, my posing as Miranda isn't the end of the world."

"Heavens, no. It was just a way of getting your foot in the door. Besides, if Redmond doesn't like your screenplay, he'll send it back and all will be forgotten."

Britt tapped her wineglass absently with her fingernail. "But what if he *does* like it?"

"Isn't that the kind of problem you'd like to have?"

Britt smiled. "You're the devil incarnate, Allison O'Donnell. You realize, don't you, that you're counseling a life of crime?"

"Hell, when you're a famous screenwriter, pulling down a million a script, I'll be able to say with satisfaction, '*I* made that woman. But for me, Britt Kingsley would still be answering phones at C.A.'"

"Yeah, but will you feel the same pride, bailing me out of jail?"

"Fear," Allison said, pointing her finger at her. "Fear."

Britt smiled. "You're probably right. This is a town of con artists and hucksters who happen to wear fifteen-hundred-dollar suits. Why should I worry if I play a little loose with the facts?"

Allison picked up her wineglass and clinked it against Britt's. "That's the spirit! Success at any price!"

They both began to laugh.

Arriving at the office the next morning, Britt prepared her script for the courier. Since she'd told Derek Redmond her name, she had to put a pseudonym on the byline. It occurred to her to use Allison's, at least for the time being. After all, her friend was virtually her partner in crime.

Once she'd typed a new title page and had the script packaged and ready to go, she took it down to the mail room with instructions to courier it to Derek Redmond's office in Westwood. Then she returned to her office to agonize. *Dream Girl* was out of her hands now. Everything was up to fate.

The phone started ringing. It seemed all Miranda's clients wanted something at the same time. For three hours they had her running. She was glad. At least it got her mind off *Dream Girl* and Derek Redmond.

Then, just before lunch, Miranda herself called from London. "Keeping the home fires burning, love?"

"I haven't let the house burn down," Britt replied, feeling a surge of guilt at the sound of her boss's voice. "At least, not yet."

"What's up?"

Britt went through the list of things that had happened. For the most part Miranda was pleased with what she'd done and had a few suggestions for follow-up. There were two clients she would call herself from London.

As Miranda rattled on, Britt had another brief urge to confess all, but then she remembered what Allison had said. Fear. She shouldn't be afraid of success. Allison had also been right when she'd argued that if Derek Redmond ended up not liking *Dream Girl,* her worries would have been for nothing. And if he did like her screenplay, well, she'd just cross that bridge when she came to it.

"I'll be visiting friends in the country for a few days," Miranda said. "Let me give you the number so you can reach me in an emergency."

Britt jotted down the number, glad that Miranda would be incommunicado for a while. That way her charade was less likely to be exposed.

They ended the conversation with Miranda assuring her that she should feel free to ring up at any time, day or night, if there was an emergency. Britt hung up, relieved that she'd gotten over another hurdle without being exposed.

A few minutes later, Sally Farland stuck her head in the door and asked if Britt wanted to go to lunch. She accepted at once. Getting away from the office would be great. Of course, lunch would be even better if she could talk about her doubts and fears with Sally, but she didn't know her well enough for that. They were friendly, but not that friendly.

Over sandwiches at the deli up the street, Britt listened to Sally lament her trials and tribulations with her boyfriend. It was a conventional tale as boyfriend stories went, but Britt did her best to be a good listener even as her mind kept turning to her own saga with Derek Redmond.

Their lunch over, Britt and Sally returned to the glass-and-steel high rise on Santa Monica Boulevard where C.A. was located. As they walked in the front door, Tiffany, a slender blonde with an affection for chewing gum, waved a message slip at Britt.

"Derek Redmond called three times while you were at lunch," the girl said. "He left messages in your voice mail but insisted I tackle you the moment you walked in. He desperately has to speak to Miranda."

Britt's heart leaped. He must have loved the script. But then she wondered what Tiffany had told him. "Did you say she was in England?"

"No, Britt, I never say anything unless I'm instructed to. All I do is connect people to the office they want and take an occasional message."

Sally took Britt's arm. "We've been caught with our pants down too often," she said as they headed for the elevator. "The assistants are the only ones besides the agents who can pass on information or answer questions. It's standard procedure."

Britt's heart was pounding as they waited for a car.

"Sounds like you've had some success," Sally said. "What's with Derek Redmond?"

"Miranda wanted me to get some information to him," Britt said nervously. "That's all." She winced, not thrilled about telling another lie. She tried to focus instead on the fact that Derek Redmond had called three times. It had to be because he loved *Dream Girl*.

Bidding Sally goodbye, Britt ran to her phone to listen to the messages Derek had left. They were brief and to the point. Tiffany was right. He urgently wanted to talk to Miranda.

Britt went into Miranda's private office, closed the door, and settled into the big leather desk chair. She shut her eyes, conjured up Miranda's voice, and took a few moments to get into character. Then she picked up the phone and dialed.

"Miranda, I want that script!" he said right out of the chute. "It's just what I've been looking for."

It took all of Britt's willpower to keep from jumping to her feet and shouting with glee. "Lovely, Derek," she managed, bouncing in her chair.

"Can we talk deal?" he asked. "You can get control of the material, can't you?"

"Well, yes, of course I can. It's just that I...er... should talk to my client a bit first. Formalities, you know." It only then occurred to her that she didn't have the slightest idea what to do next. Did she—that is, C.A.—draw up a contract, or did Derek Redmond? Clearly she wasn't prepared.

"This Allison O'Donnell has real talent," Derek went on. "I'm eager to meet her."

"Uh...yes, she's...a lovely girl."

"I don't care what she looks like, Miranda. I don't even care about her disposition. She writes a damned good script and that's all that matters."

"Right you are, Derek." Britt couldn't help tittering, but it was more from nerves than anything else. "Shall I prepare the...uh, usual formalities?" she ventured, not knowing what else to say.

"Let's don't worry about that yet," he said. "The first thing I want to do is meet with your client. There are a few things in the script I'd like to discuss."

"What sort of things?"

"Just some ideas I have, possibly some changes to consider."

"I see." Britt felt her euphoria falter.

"Nothing big," he hastily added. "But I like to run my ideas past the writer. I don't believe anything worthy can be written by committee. Collaboration is the name of the game."

"Quite right," Britt said, fumbling.

"Since you and I haven't met, why don't the three of us get together? We could do lunch tomorrow, or better yet, breakfast. I like to get an early start."

Britt's mind started spinning. There was no way she could meet with him! Good heavens, what had she gotten herself into? "Uh...that would be delightful..." she stammered, struggling to focus her thoughts. "But I do need to talk to Allison. Can I ring you back, love?"

"Sure, Miranda. I'm doing lunch today with a friend, but I'll be in my office from three on."

"Okay, well, talk to you soon, then, Derek, love." Britt hung up the phone and let her head drop right down on the desk. "Lord," she mumbled. "Just strike me with a lightning bolt and get it over with."

4

Derek Redmond left his office in Westwood and drove east on Wilshire until he came to Santa Monica Boulevard. He pulled into the Peninsula Beverly Hills Hotel, left his Porsche 911 with the valet parking attendant, and went inside. He breezed through the lobby.

"Mr. Redmond," a voice called from the direction of the reception desk.

He glanced over as an assistant manager made his way toward him, smiling.

"Good to see you," the man, a young sophisticated European, said in a cordial tone. "Will we be serving you in the Belvedere this afternoon?"

"I'm meeting Oliver Wheatley for lunch."

"Oh, yes, sir, of course. Mr. Wheatley's poolside. I'll have you shown to his cabana." The assistant manager signaled for a bellhop, who promptly joined them and was told to take Derek to Oliver Wheatley's cabana.

They took the elevator to the rooftop pool, which had become the latest deal-making meeting place for Hollywood moguls. Derek was more into making pictures than doing the Hollywood scene, but a certain amount of schmoozing was unavoidable. That meant putting in time at places like this. One modest hit under his belt and another in the can and ready to be released had not exactly made him a power to be reckoned with, but he no longer had to sit in outer offices by the hour, waiting to see someone with juice. He'd done breakfast or lunch in the Peninsula's Club Bar a couple of times, but this was his first trip to the rooftop pool.

Oliver had told Derek on the phone that morning that he was working on putting together a three-picture package and was up to his ears in lawyers and accountants, but he'd be taking a break around lunchtime and would enjoy seeing him. Derek had been glad to accept.

Like a lot of Brits who'd come to California to make films, Oliver didn't fit the typical Hollywood tycoon mold, either, but his successes of the last few years had, by his own reckoning, "sucked him into the game." For reasons Derek wasn't entirely sure about, Oliver had taken him under his wing and acted as a mentor. In fact, he'd been helpful in getting the package together for *Code Red*.

They arrived at the hotel rooftop and Derek looked out at the pool area, squinting in the bright sunshine. Then he slipped his sunglasses down from where he'd pushed them into his dark hair, so that he could take in the scene.

There was the usual assortment of bikini-clad girls sunning themselves in deck chairs or wading in the pool. There were also a few young bronze studs, but it was quickly obvious that all the important action was taking place in the canvas cabanas surrounding the pool. As he strode past them, Derek could hear the clatter of fax machines and the sound of cellular phones ringing. It was a circuslike atmosphere, but instead of greasepaint the performers were wearing jeans, polo shirts, Carrera sunglasses, and fifteen-thousand-dollar gold watches.

As he came to Oliver's cabana, Derek found him in a lounge chair, a cellular phone to his ear and Meg, his dark-haired, middle-aged secretary, beside him with a laptop computer nearby. Oliver, in his mid-forties, was wearing Bermuda shorts and a short-sleeved silk shirt. Noticing Derek, he gave him a wave and beckoned him to enter. Derek handed the bellhop a couple of bucks and stepped into the cabana's shady interior. Meg smiled up at him.

Oliver, who was a bit on the portly side and had very pink skin, finished up his call and extended his hand. "You made it, old bean. Come sit down. I'm ready to take a break from this insanity." He turned to the secretary. "Meg, why don't you go have some lunch? We'll start again in an hour's time."

"Yes, sir."

"Oh, and send a waiter over so Derek and I can order something to eat, if you would, please."

She nodded and left. Derek took the chair she'd vacated. Oliver lay back in the lounge chair, his hands clasped behind his head as he surveyed the panorama of pool and sky. Two young women in bikinis paraded by. Derek watched Oliver follow their progress.

"Incredible, isn't it?" Oliver said, smiling. "Sometimes I'm embarrassed to admit I've been seduced by it."

"Everything's relative," Derek said.

"Relative to what?"

"No matter what kind of life a person leads, now and then you have to stop and ask yourself what it's all about."

"Oh, gawd, a philosopher. I didn't know there were any in this country."

Derek chuckled. "I guess what I'm saying, Oliver, is I try not to get too caught up in all this. The biggest mistake people in this town make is taking themselves too seriously."

"You don't, evidently."

"I'm into my work. Or at least I like to think so."

"That's not taking yourself seriously?"

Derek stared abstractedly. "I suppose it is, in a way. But I don't regard this as the real world," he said, waving his hand toward the scene before them.

Oliver didn't say anything for a while. "Maybe I don't, either, Derek. When I'm home in England, this place seems more like a dream. And when I'm here I feel like I'm on holiday, a great long one."

A long-legged blond beauty in a thong bikini climbed from the pool right in front of them. She smiled in their direction before padding off.

"There's something to be said for living out one's fantasies, however," Oliver said with a laugh.

The waiter came and took their orders for lunch. After he'd left, Derek said, "I owe you thanks, by the way."

"How's that?" Oliver asked, draining the last of a fruit drink that had been sitting on the table beside him.

"Miranda Maxwell was kind enough to put me onto a wonderful script by an unknown screenwriter. It's a bit rough but there's a real freshness to the writing."

"Miranda has judgment," Oliver said. "It's her best quality, in my opinion."

"How is she to deal with? Pretty straight?"

"Oh, Miranda's a straight shooter, all right. She won't make any promises she can't keep or representations she can't back up. She's a love."

"I'm looking forward to dealing with her," Derek said. "She's trying to set up a meeting for tomorrow with her client. Hopefully the three of us will get together for breakfast and hammer things out."

"Breakfast? Has the Concorde started flying to L.A. without me knowing about it?"

"What do you mean?"

"Miranda's in London. Has been for a week."

Derek looked at him, perplexed. "Oliver, what are you saying? I've talked to Miranda in her office several times over the past couple of days."

Oliver shook his head. "Couldn't have, old man. Miranda's in London. Trust me. I've spoken with her twice this morning. Conference calls. Had trouble hooking up the London link. The operator had to go through the business three or four times to get it right. Miranda said it was probably the bloody fog. Said the whole town was swimming in the stuff. She must have rung you up and you assumed she was in L.A. Happened to me once. Talked to a bleeding lawyer for half an hour, thinking he was across town. Turned out the sod was in Rome with his mistress, probably eating grapes from her navel while talking to me." Oliver laughed.

Derek scratched his head. He tried to recall the circumstances of his conversations with Miranda. He was certain he'd dialed C.A. and had been put right through to her. Or could her assistant have patched him through to London? No, that made no sense. When he'd proposed breakfast, Miranda would have said she was in London and couldn't meet with him. He wondered what the hell was going on. Something was fishy.

"Oliver, is it possible Miranda spoke with me from London, but didn't want me to know that's where she was?"

"Whatever for?"

Derek stroked his chin, considering the situation as the waiter arrived with the fresh order of fruit drinks. The man went off and Oliver raised his glass.

"Cheers."

Derek ruminated. "Somebody's smoking something, Oliver. Could it be one of us, or is it Miranda?"

"Ah, a philosopher *and* a skeptic. What say we ring Miranda up in London and ask her what gives?"

"No, don't bother her. I'm sure it's a misunderstanding."

"Balderdash! You've got me curious." Oliver reached for his cellular phone, holding it up for Derek to see as he dialed. "Note the international code." Then he sat back and waited. "Hello," he said airily, "Oliver Wheatley here. Miss Maxwell, please.... Oh? She's not in, then? She wouldn't have gone off to America, would she?... The country, you say. Has she been gone long?... Left an hour ago? I see. You're the housekeeper, are you?... And what's your name, love?... Priscilla? Smashing. We've a wee problem, Priscilla. I'm a client of Miranda's and ringing up from California. I've a gentleman here with me from the FBI. That's the American Scotland Yard. We're investigating a case of mistaken identity and we'd like to confirm where Miss Maxwell's been for the past few days. Would you be kind enough to tell Mr. Ness where Miss Maxwell has been, say, the last few days?... That's a love." Grinning, Oliver handed the phone to Derek.

"Hello," he said in his best Kevin Costner voice, "this is Elliot Ness. Sorry to trouble you, Priscilla, but if you could just verify that Miss Maxwell has been in London the past few days."

"Oh, yes, sir," the woman assured. "She would have been here at her town house Monday a week. But an hour ago she did leave for the country, sir. If it's urgent, I can give you the number there and you can ring her. You might wish to allow an hour or two, though.

The traffic's bad on the M-5 and, well, she'd likely have stopped for her supper on the way.''

"Oh, that won't be necessary," he said. "This is just a routine inquiry."

"Are you certain, sir?"

"Quite sure. You don't have to trouble Miss Maxwell with this. Everything is quite satisfactory. Thank you very much." Derek pushed the Off button, then handed the phone back to Oliver, who was beaming.

"Are you the one who's been smoking, laddie?" Oliver asked.

"Could be a suspect as yet unnamed," Derek replied. "I should be having some interesting phone calls this afternoon."

"Be certain to let me know what's happening, Mr. Ness. Sounds like you have a very interesting case on your hands."

Derek Redmond picked up his glass and took a swig of juice. "Let me put it this way. Breakfast tomorrow could prove to be very interesting."

Britt closed the last of the client files on her desk and returned the stack to the file cabinet in Miranda's office. She checked her watch and decided it was time to call Derek Redmond. Closing the door and taking her place at Miranda's desk, she took a deep breath and slowly exhaled as she conjured up Miranda in her mind. When she was satisfied she was fixed on the right character, she dialed the number to Derek's office. After a brief delay he came onto the line.

"Miranda," he said cheerily, "were you able to talk to your client?"

"Yes, Allison would be pleased to meet you for breakfast, Derek. She's terribly excited."

"Terrific. Will you be joining us?"

"I would, love, but I've got other commitments. Early-morning powwow over at Disney."

"What a shame. I was really hoping we could get together. I find it much easier talking to someone after meeting face-to-face. But I guess it won't hurt if Allison and I meet first."

"Not in the least, Derek. She'd be delighted, believe me."

"Can you have her at the Polo Lounge at, say, eight tomorrow morning?"

"She'll be there with bells on her toes. I promise."

"Terrific," he said. "I'm looking forward to it. I'll give you a jingle after Allison and I talk."

"I'll be eager to hear how it goes," she said.

"Yes, it seems to me you said something about having to go to London soon. When do you plan on leaving?"

Britt gulped, thinking quickly. "Uh . . . not for a few days, anyway. I've a couple of things to finish up before I'm off. One of which, if all goes well, will be doing a deal with you, Derek."

"I'm sure we'll have the pleasure. I can't tell you how much I'm looking forward to it."

"*Ciao,* love." Britt hung up the phone, clenching her fist in triumph. It was easier than she'd thought.

"Bloody hell!" she exclaimed and spun the desk chair around, giggling gleefully.

There was a light rap on the door, bringing her celebration to an abrupt halt. She got out of Miranda's chair and went to see who was there. It was Sally, with an inquisitive look on her face.

"Everything all right?" she asked. "You weren't at your desk and I saw the door closed. I...uh...thought maybe—"

"Oh, I was on the phone," Britt said. "I wanted a little privacy because..." She hesitated, feeling another lie forming on her lips. She tried to find a way to avoid it, but couldn't come up with anything truthful, yet safe. "Because, uh, I was talking to my doctor," she finally blurted.

"Oh. Aren't you feeling well?"

Britt swallowed hard. "I'm okay," she said, "but tomorrow morning I have a doctor's appointment. He wanted me to come in. I'll be late for work."

"No problem," Sally replied. "I'll have Miranda's calls routed to my phone. I'll cover for you until you get in."

"That would be great," Britt said. "I don't think I'll be too late."

"Well, the reason I dropped by," Sally continued, "is that Joyce Wilson is on the warpath again about the British getting special treatment in Hollywood. Gordon ran into her last night at Spago and she had a few choice barbs for Miranda. She blames her for sabotaging her interview with Westley Asquith."

"Rightly so," Britt said.

"Yes, well, Gordon thought you ought to be on your toes and aware."

"Thanks, I'll give Westley's publicist another call. I'm sure that's what Miranda would do. And the next time I talk to her, I'll mention what Gordon said."

Sally patted Britt on the arm. "You're getting the hang of the business real fast."

Britt smiled, but felt like a terrible hypocrite. She liked C.A. and she was uncomfortable about having used Miranda, although she wouldn't allow her boss to be hurt. On the contrary, once she became one of the leading screenwriters in Hollywood, she'd want Miranda to represent her—assuming she was willing.

Of course, that was a bit premature. Right now her most pressing concern was her meeting with Derek Redmond. It still hadn't sunk in completely, but one of Hollywood's up-and-coming directors loved her script! Maybe, at long last, her time had come!

5

A few minutes before eight the next morning Britt turned off Sunset Boulevard and drove up the palm-lined drive of the Beverly Hills Hotel—the "Pink Palace," as the locals called it. She had passed by the place many times, and had often wondered if she'd ever be inside, wheeling and dealing with the big boys. Now her chance had come and she was thrilled.

The Polo Lounge was one of the primo meeting places of the Hollywood moguls and had been for over fifty years. She figured that Derek Redmond had probably picked it to impress her, which was fine by her. Negotiating her first deal under the watchful eye of the ghosts of Darryl Zanuck, Spencer Tracy, Walt Disney and all the other old polo players who haunted the place was as good a way to begin as any.

Ignoring the valets, Britt drove past the entrance and went on to the parking lot. Aspiring screenwriters in six-year-old Toyotas couldn't throw money around like a celebrity. Besides, this wasn't her turf. She was a guest, and glad for once to be able to behave like the humble person she was.

Of course, it was unfortunate that she'd be meeting Derek Redmond under an assumed identity, but Britt was relieved that she wouldn't be playing a role, as well—like she had on the phone when she'd pretended to be Miranda. For this meeting, she could answer questions honestly and be candid when discussing her craft. She'd be herself—in all but her true name, of course.

Britt got out of her car and locked it. She smoothed her lightweight navy knit dress that nicely showed her curves. Her heels made her legs look great. Her honey-colored hair hung straight to her shoulders. Her only jewelry was a pair of chunky fake gold earrings. No rings, bracelets or necklaces. The overall effect was attractive without being flashy.

She'd considered dressing down to minimize her sex appeal but she liked flattering clothes and always bought the best that she could afford, although her budget was modest. Besides, she knew she had a good figure and great legs. Still, this was an extraordinary situation and she wanted to project the right image. Maybe she should have made an exception and gone really conservative, but it was too late now.

Walking toward the entrance of the hotel, Britt was nervous. This was the worst case of stage fright she'd ever had. How many times did someone like her, a real unknown, get an opportunity like this? She knew she had to stay focused, ignore things like the way the valets were eyeing her.

Britt stepped inside the hotel and glanced about the lobby, immediately noticing the entrance to the Polo Lounge. Several middle-aged men and one woman were waiting near the maître d's podium, but none of them looked familiar. Derek Redmond's dark good looks from the pictures she'd seen of him were emblazoned on her brain, although the image may have been embellished some by her fantasies of him. She hoped she would like him, that he would be a nice man. But all that really mattered was that he wanted to turn her screenplay into a movie.

Standing at the rear of the small crowd, she waited for her turn. When the leader of the group completed his conversation with the hostess, the people moved to the side and Britt stepped forward.

"May I help you?" the stately woman behind the podium asked.

"I'm meeting Derek Redmond," Britt replied.

"Oh, yes, Miss O'Donnell. Mr. Redmond is waiting for you in the Loggia. This way, please."

They went through the Green room with the telephone-equipped booths, many of them in use. There was a low buzz of activity. Gray-haired men in Italian suits and younger men with sunglasses pushed up in their hair glanced at her as she passed by, if they weren't too engrossed in conversation.

Judging by the looks she was getting, people were wondering whose bimbo she might be. That had to be their conclusion. She didn't have a famous face and she was too young to be one of the industry's female movers and shakers. In Hollywood, that left only one category.

Never mind, Britt told herself. One day she'd be known by the insiders as a great writing talent. She'd be recognized for her ability and achievements.

The hostess took her into the quiet inner sanctum of the Loggia where, according to Allison, the really big mucky-mucks did their megamillion wheeling and dealing, especially during breakfast. Britt felt a swell of pride. It was the first time since she'd been in L.A. that didn't feel like an outsider with her nose to the glass, looking in.

She glanced at the sober-faced, affluent people occupying the booths. She could smell the money and power, but didn't recognize anyone. Allison had told her the crowd would be mostly the less well-known, but terribly powerful money people and industry execs. "The stars don't get up that early, kiddo, so don't expect to see Tom Cruise."

Britt was shown to one of the lesser booths in the corner, where Derek Redmond sat waiting.

"Miss O'Donnell has arrived, Mr. Redmond," the hostess said pleasantly as she stepped aside, smiling at each of them in turn.

Britt, covering her awe as best she could, watched him as he checked her out. Then Derek slid from the booth and extended his hand before she could say a word. He looked like his pictures, but the flesh-and-blood presence was even better looking than she'd anticipated. She was actually a bit stunned, not expecting him to have the effect on her that he did.

He was lean and muscular, with longish straight black hair and clear green eyes. He had a sensitive face, and yet there was a manliness about him, too. He was wearing an open-necked shirt under a sports coat and round wire-rimmed glasses that gave him an almost-intellectual look, although he had an easy, casual manner.

"Allison," he said, "it's an honor to meet you. I'm a big fan, if Miranda hasn't already told you."

She left her hand resting in his as she looked into his green eyes. "Thank you. I'm a fan of yours, as well, Mr. Redmond."

"Derek," he said warmly, still holding her hand.

He had an engaging smile and a warm, charming manner that seemed genuine. The line between self-confidence and arrogance was narrow. First impressions put him on the right side of it. At one level she'd been prepared for him, though not quite the way she found him. She realized that she was reacting to him as a man, which was not at all what she'd had in mind.

"Well, come sit down," he said, taking her arm.

Britt slipped into the booth on the side opposite where he'd been sitting. "I hope I'm not too late," she said.

"Not at all. You're right on time." He took his place.

They looked at each other for what seemed like a very long time. Britt was feeling something—an awareness—that she knew she shouldn't. Derek Redmond seemed to be peering right inside her as though he were searching for something. She knew her hands were trembling, but she didn't dare look down at them to confirm it.

"I loved your screenplay, Allison," he said.

His words thrilled her. "I'm glad you liked it."

He went on, discussing what he liked about her writing and the kinds of scripts he liked to direct.

Britt listened, mesmerized. She couldn't recall ever having felt such a deep and compelling rapport with someone so quickly. Usually it took hours of conversation—hours of feeling someone out—before common links were discovered.

"Why did you decide to do a screenplay? Why not a novel?" he asked, curious.

"I suppose because I'm visual and my background—limited though it is—is acting. I visualize raw material for actors and actresses to do their thing."

"And directors," he said.

"Yes, directors of course—foremost, I suppose."

Derek stared at her mouth, taking her in as his eyes moved over her. It was an appreciative appraisal, but not a salacious one. He might have been evaluating her for a lighting effect or a camera angle. Whatever was going on in his mind, she read admiration on his face.

"I've a confession to make," he said. "Not many directors like to admit this, but there are scripts that almost direct themselves. When you read the script and it's good, you're able to visualize the whole thing as though the film has already been made and you're simply watching it. That's what happened to me when I read *Dream Girl*.''

"That's a very nice thing to say, but you're discounting your importance."

"You're saying even a good script can be bungled."

"I'm saying there's a big step from script to the screen. Michelangelo believed his sculptures were already fully formed in the block of marble and his task was to liberate the figure from the stone. But I'm not willing to give the marble that much credit,'' she added with a laugh.

"Your script is a good deal more to me than a block of stone is to a sculptor, Allison. But the comparison is flattering. Thank you."

Britt beamed, incredibly happy.

"You know," he said, "*Dream Girl* is the sort of script I've tried to describe. It works in my mind. I really want to make it into a film."

"I hope you do."

He reached across the table and took her hand. "I fully intend to, believe me."

She glanced down at the hand that unconsciously caressed hers as he gazed at her with intensity. The affection, unconscious or not, flustered her. "Miranda said you wanted some changes, though."

Derek gave her hand a final squeeze before removing his. "There are always little things, sequences or transitions you see a bit differently than what's in the script. It's almost an editing function."

"Miranda gave me the impression it might be more than that."

He shrugged. "I want to play with the ending. I haven't decided how I feel about it, exactly, but it's something we can talk about."

Britt shrugged. "Sure."

"There were two principal writers on *Code Red* and before it was over, I was practically a member of the writing team. While I like to work closely with writers on changes, I don't see this film going the same way. Thrillers are a different kettle of fish."

Britt wasn't sure if he saw a problem and was trying to play it down, or if he was assuring her that his concerns were minor. For the first time she began to sense he was giving her a sales pitch and that made her wonder.

"So, what's the bottom line?" she asked.

"If I do the film, I'd like to have you as a member of the team—helping me to fine-tune it. The actors will be critical, as well."

"That sounds good to me."

"And what if our visions diverge?"

Britt studied him. "You're asking if I can be a good soldier."

"I'm asking if you can be a team player."

"And recognize who's in command," she added.

"I wouldn't put it that way, exactly."

She pondered his point. "I'm a rookie, I know," she said, "but I'm familiar enough with the business to know a writer has to let go at a certain point."

"Good. I wanted us to be clear, to get everything on the table up front. The fewer surprises, the better."

"I appreciate that," she said. "I really do."

Derek nodded as though he'd heard what he wanted. "I like the feel of this," he said, gesturing back and forth between them. "Do you?"

Britt knew he was talking about their collaboration on *Dream Girl*, but she couldn't help considering the question another way, too. They were two people who'd been finding common ground over something they both felt passionate about. She'd never experienced that before.

Britt didn't realize it, but she was staring at him, her mouth slightly agape. All kinds of crazy and wonderful notions streamed through her mind, thoughts and feelings she'd never experienced before, a quiet excitement that was new to her.

"Allison?"

"Huh?"

"Is this feeling good?"

She blinked. "Oh...uh...yes. I like your philosophy."

"Can you live with it?"

She shrugged. "Sure."

She wasn't going to tell him, but he probably could have made chaining her to the wall and facing a cat-o'-nine-tails part of the deal. Derek probably knew it, too, but it said something about him that he could refrain from being pushy.

"Good," he said, beaming. "That gets us over the first hurdle." He signaled the waiter. "And now, how about some breakfast?"

Britt was feeling so amenable that he could have said, "And now, how about a dip in the pool?" and she would have agreed.

"Sounds good," she said.

Derek recommended the Dutch apple pancakes for which the Polo Lounge was famous, and although a glass of juice and a slice of dry toast was a more typical breakfast for her, Britt ordered the pancakes. After the waiter had gone, she glanced around the room, taking it in for the first time since sitting down.

"This is my first meal in the Polo Lounge," she said.

"I thought it might be appropriate, considering we're here to wheel and deal."

"Somehow I don't think my little screenplay is in the same league with what's going on at the other tables."

Derek looked around himself. "A lot of these folks are strangers to me, as well, but there are at least two network entertainment-division heads who I recognize. I assume they're talking deals."

"For millions, I imagine."

"Many millions."

Britt felt her pulse jump up a beat or two.

"That silver-haired gentleman in the booth with the man and woman is Jack Valenti, head of the Motion Picture Association of America."

"Oh, yes, I recognize him now."

"Care to meet him?" Derek asked, cocking his brow whimsically.

Britt looked at him questioningly. "Do you know him?"

"No, I was just kidding. In fact, if you want to know the truth, this group is out of my league. I'm still triple A, but with major-league potential."

"It's nice you can admit that. There's a lot of pretense in this town and precious little humility."

"Honesty has always felt better to me than trying to be something I'm not. Maybe it's the way I was raised."

His words stabbed at her like a knife.

"So tell me, Allison, how and where did you come to know Miranda?" he asked.

The question was uncannily ironic. She looked into his clear green eyes, and a terrible urge welled up in her to blurt out the truth. The first words—"I'm not Allison O'Donnell. My name is Britt Kingsley and I've deceived you"—were forming on her lips when she swallowed them, choking them off.

"I met her through a friend," she said shamefully. "Somebody who knew someone who worked for one of the other agents at C.A."

Derek nodded. "Miranda's an interesting lady, isn't she?"

Britt's cheeks had to have turned a blistering red. The worst part was knowing she had nobody to blame but herself. "Yes, very interesting," she replied.

"So you haven't known her long, then?"

"I've only seen her a few times," she said, agonizing with each additional lie.

The trouble was, if she stopped now, before the deal was done, everything could go down the drain. Just a few more hours and it would be over. Once it was safe to come out in the open, she'd find a way to make amends and clear her conscience; she promised herself that.

"Have you met with Miranda at C.A.?" Derek asked. "Or somewhere else?"

His tone was nonchalant, his manner conversational, but even so, the question struck her as curious. Could he be suspicious? A tremor went through her at the thought. "Not in the office," she told him, sensing it was the thing to say. "Why do you ask?"

He shrugged. "I was curious. I haven't met Miranda face-to-face yet, but I hope to soon. Naturally, she's the one I'll have to work out the deal with."

Britt managed to smile, covering the horror she felt. "I don't imagine I could relay any messages or anything."

"No, you don't want to get involved in the messy stuff. The reason you have an agent is to protect you. Besides, she'd kill me if I tried to cut her out of the loop."

"I'm sure that's not true."

"Well, it's your first deal, so let's do it by the book."

Britt groaned inwardly. "Whatever you think."

The waiter came with two enormous glasses of orange juice. Although it was eight-thirty in the morning, Britt almost wished there was a shot of vodka in it. She could have used something to settle her nerves.

"Ah," Derek said, "my favorite beverage."

He picked up his glass and extended it, offering to touch it to hers. Britt took hers, suddenly so shaky she was afraid she'd drop it.

"To *Dream Girl*," he toasted. "And to you, Allison. Here's hoping you're the dream writer I've been looking for."

Britt managed to return his smile, but it was all she could do to keep from bursting into tears. The weight of every bad deed she'd ever done pressed down on her.

Lowering her glass, she scooted to the edge of the banquette. "Will you excuse me, Derek," she said. "I'll be back in just a minute."

He started to get up, but she motioned for him to stay seated. He reached out and grasped her hand, stopping her from leaving.

"Allison," he said, "I'm going to give Miranda a buzz on my cellular phone and tell her to draw up an option agreement. I've decided there's no need to drag this out. You and I are going to do *Dream Girl*, and it's going to be one of the biggest hits of the year."

Britt's heart soared. But her guilty conscience brought it right back down. Tears bubbled from her eyes. She mouthed the words, "Thank you," and turned, practically running from the room.

6

Derek watched Allison O'Donnell leave. He had no idea what to make of her or the situation. But one thing was certain—he found her fascinating. She was damned attractive. The heads she turned were evidence of that. Yet more than the physical beauty, he found himself attracted to her as a person. Things had really clicked between them. He'd never experienced that before—at least not so dramatically, and not in the same way.

Of course, there was still the matter of the hoax involving Miranda Maxwell. He assumed that Allison was involved in some way. He had briefly considered the possibility that she too was a victim, but it was hard to believe that a third party would have anything to gain by trying to deceive both Allison and him.

But why they'd resorted to such a grand deception wasn't clear. The screenplay was real enough. He had no doubt that Allison had written it because it would be impossible to fake the conversation they'd just had. Still, something was fishy and he was determined to get to the bottom of it.

He knew he had to be careful. The last thing he wanted to do was alienate her—he had as much at stake as she. First and foremost, there was *Dream Girl* to consider. He wanted to make it into a movie.

He took his cellular phone from the briefcase and dialed C.A., asking the receptionist for Miranda Maxwell's office.

"Neither Ms. Maxwell nor her assistant are in today," the woman said. "I can connect you to Miranda's voice mail, or if you'd prefer, Mr. Mallik's assistant can help you."

"That's all right. Just have Miranda telephone me as soon as you can, will you, please? This is Derek Redmond."

"Yes, sir."

"Thanks."

He disconnected the call and put away the phone. Then he pondered the situation. It had all the earmarks of some kind of a con game, but the motive eluded him. The key had to be the imitation Miranda Maxwell. That was who he had to get to.

Britt came out of the ladies' room and headed back to the dining room. Passing a pay phone, she suddenly remembered that Derek was going to phone Miranda. She wondered if Tiffany would have put the call through to Sally, and if so, what Sally had said to him. Maybe she should find out before returning to the table.

Britt put a quarter in the telephone and dialed C.A. "Tiffany," she said when the receptionist answered, "this is Britt. Have there been any calls for Miranda?"

"Yes, Derek Redmond called a few minutes ago."

"Did you put him through to Sally?"

"No, he just said he wanted Miranda to call. I thought I'd let you handle it. Will you be in soon?"

"No, I'm going to be tied up a while longer. Would you put me through to Sally, please?"

"Sure."

"Sally," Britt said when her friend came on the line, "I need to get ahold of Derek Redmond for Miranda. Is there a way you can get his cellular number for me?"

"I suppose so, but it'll take me a minute. Want to hold?"

"Yes."

Britt waited, agonizing. Things were getting more and more complicated. She didn't know why that should surprise her. Once you started lying you got sucked in deeper and deeper. The only question was whether she could keep her head above water long enough to get Derek on the dotted line.

As she waited, she pictured his smiling face. The man was incredibly handsome—sexy and intelligent, sensitive and yet strong. She felt one of those intense, physical attractions that she wrote about, the kind that left her heroines numb. That tug in the gut was the most wonderful feeling in the world. What a shame the first guy in years to do that to her should be Derek Redmond, of all people. She was already playing a dangerous game.

"Britt," Sally said, coming back on the line, "I've got it." She read off the number and Britt jotted it down on a scrap of paper she took from her purse.

"Thanks," she said. "You're a lifesaver."

"What's going on, anyway? I thought you were at the doctor's."

"I am. I just remembered I had to make this call for Miranda. Oh, and Sally..."

"Yes?"

"If Derek should happen to call in and you talk to him, don't mention that Miranda's in England, okay?"

"Why not?"

"Let's just say Miranda didn't want him to know."

Sally sighed. "All right. I assume you know what you're doing."

Britt hung up, then glanced around to make sure no one was within hearing. She closed her eyes for a minute to conjure up Miranda. Then she dialed the number Sally had given her. The phone rang several times before he answered.

"Derek, darling, Miranda Maxwell here. I understand you wanted to speak with me."

"Yes, I did. Thanks for returning the call."

"What's up?"

"I'm meeting with Allison and we're hitting it off real well. I wanted you to know."

Britt beamed happily. "That's fabulous, dear. I couldn't be more pleased."

"I think we'll be able to work together," he said. "In fact I'm sure of it. She's bright, engaging. It's love at first sight."

She almost jumped for joy. "That's smashing, Derek! You've made my day."

"Hold on a second," he said.

Britt waited a few seconds, then he came back on the line.

"Listen, Miranda, can I call you right back? I've got to take care of something here. Are you in your office?"

"No, as a matter of fact I'm out doing breakfast myself."

"Do you have a number where I can reach you? It'll be just a minute or two."

Britt did a quick calculation. "I can wait here a few moments, Derek, but not long."

"Give me the number."

"It's 555-4839," she said, reading the number off the pay phone.

"I'll get right back to you."

Britt hung up, wondering what that was all about. Had somebody come to the table? She considered going to have a look, but was afraid someone might try to use the phone in her absence. She stood waiting and after another thirty seconds the phone rang.

"Hello."

"It's me, Derek," he said.

"Yes, dear."

"Listen, I want to get together with you as soon as possible to discuss *Dream Girl,*" he told her. "Do you have plans for dinner this evening?"

"This evening? I'm afraid I do have an engagement. Sorry."

"How does tomorrow look?"

Britt gulped. She knew she couldn't put him off forever and it sounded like he was determined. "My schedule is just rotten this week, love."

"We really need to discuss the option agreement."

Britt felt sick. It wasn't going to be as easy wrapping this up as she'd hoped. "I'd be delighted to sit down with you in good time, Derek, dear, but there's really no reason to hold things up until we do. Why don't I give you a jingle tomorrow, and we can discuss the option. You know, it won't come cheap."

He hesitated before answering. "Yes, there won't be any problem there. I want the film."

"Then let's do a deal, by all means. Will you be in your office in the morning?"

"More likely at home."

"I'll ring you up as soon as the fog lifts, as it were."

"Okay. I look forward to hearing from you, Miranda."

"Until tomorrow, then, dear." Britt hung up, relieved. What if he'd insisted on negotiating in person? That would have been a disaster. Of course, she wasn't off the hook yet. Things could still blow up in her face. She sighed and headed for the dining room. The wages of sin.

Derek was sipping orange juice when he saw Allison enter the room. She walked toward him with the long graceful strides of a model. She was attractive without being flashy. Hollywood was full of gorgeous women, but there was something about this one—the way she moved, the intelligence in her eyes.... It was hard to put his finger on it. They had a lot in common, although it was too early to say he knew her. But he *wanted* to know her. That much was certain.

As she slid into the booth, he noticed the faintest sign of worry on her brow. When she saw that their breakfasts had been served, she protested.

"Derek, you shouldn't have waited for me. Sorry I was so long."

"No problem. I was on the phone, as a matter of fact. Doing a little business."

The waiter, who'd left the plate covers on to keep the pancakes warm, came over and removed them. Derek watched her lean over to inhale the aroma of the food, catching her eye. Her cheeks colored as she smiled.

"Smells good," she said.

There was a mischievousness about her. He liked that. Yet, a part of him wasn't quite sure how far to trust her, considering the hoax. He decided to hold back a bit, at least until he was sure what was going on.

"I spoke to Miranda," he said, as he watched her pour maple syrup over her cakes.

"Oh? What did she have to say?"

"We agreed to work out a deal for *Dream Girl.*"

Britt grinned. "Was she pleased?"

"I think so. But she seems to be having a little trouble finding time to meet with me." He took a sip of coffee.

"Miranda's an odd duck, Derek, and really busy. But I'm sure she's eager to do the deal. She damned well better be!" She smiled and took a bite of her Dutch apple pancakes.

"You know, you sounded like her just then, the way you said, 'odd duck' and 'damned well better be.'"

Allison blinked, then smoothly said, "Accents are contagious. We were talking about Miranda and that made me think about her voice, I guess. I just love the way the English talk, don't you?"

"I suppose." He studied her face, liking what he saw very much, even if he knew she'd gotten herself mixed up in something fishy.

Color came to her cheeks as he watched her munching. He put some syrup on his cakes. This game they were playing was getting more interesting all the time. He was eager to see what would happen next.

The waiter came with more coffee. Allison picked up her cup, holding it with both hands as she looked across the table at him. He evaluated what he was feeling for her and found it as remarkable as it was simulating.

"What are you doing for lunch, Allison?" he asked.

"Lunch?" She blinked. "I haven't finished breakfast."

"I know, but I like to plan ahead."

She threw back her head and laughed. There was a joy about her that he loved.

"You aren't serious," she said.

"Of course, I'm serious. I think we should do lunch, further explore our collaborative relationship." He eyed her, waiting to see her reaction.

"I'm supposed to work today."

"You get sick days, don't you? Where does your employer think you are, anyway?"

"I said I had a doctor's appointment."

"Couldn't the shot he gave you have made you sick?"

"You're counseling crime, Derek."

"I feel like playing hooky and would like company. What would you say to a drive up the coast and having a leisurely lunch along the way?"

She leaned her elbows on the table, resting her chin on her hands. "What exactly did you have in mind?"

"A drive, lunch, conversation."

"Is that all?"

"Should there be something else?" he asked.

She shifted uncomfortably. "I've been in Hollywood long enough to know that sometimes there are...expectations."

"I'm not propositioning you, if that's what you're concerned about. If that's what I had in mind, I'd say so."

"Being the supplicant in this situation, I tend to be a little paranoid."

"Let me reassure you. I don't make sex a condition of my professional relationships. My interest in *Dream Girl* is quite separate from my interest in you. As far as

I'm concerned we're going to do the picture, Allison. Whether we do lunch today or at any other time is up to you—unconditionally.''

"I like your attitude, Mr. Redmond," she said. "And I appreciate it."

He took a bite of pancake as he regarded her, feeling the energy flow back and forth between them. She wasn't afraid to look him in the eye. He liked that. He took another sip of coffee.

"I don't pretend to be a Boy Scout or a monk, however," he said.

Allison lifted a brow. "Is that a warning?"

"More a disclaimer."

"And what are you disclaiming?"

He smiled, looking her in the eye. "I can't promise not to enjoy your company, even if I manage to behave myself."

"My, all this candor is unexpected."

"Aren't you used to men being straight with you?"

"No, not most of the time."

"Then I'll try not to disappoint you," he said, as he reached across the table and took her hand. "Respect—and by that I mean mutual respect—is an important part of every friendship, Allison."

"Do you mean that, or is it just a fancy line?"

"The proof will be in the pudding."

"What you're saying is that if I want to find out, I'm going to have to take a chance."

"Ultimately every relationship is a matter of trust. You have to trust me. I have to trust you. We both have to trust Miranda."

She flushed. If he didn't know better, he'd have said he was seeing guilt at work. He rubbed the back of her hand with his thumb, noticing that she wasn't looking him in the eye now as she had earlier. He decided they were likely in for a very interesting afternoon.

Britt knew the last thing she ought to be doing was running off with Derek Redmond for a carefree afternoon, but she'd agreed to do just that. He was suspicious, that much she could tell. But what she didn't know was what, exactly, he suspected. Her task for the afternoon would be to put his mind at ease.

Before leaving the Polo Lounge, Britt called Sally and told her she wasn't well and wouldn't be returning to the office. Then she went with Derek in his Porsche, driving west on Sunset Boulevard toward the coast.

From time to time she glanced over at him, watching the breeze from the sunroof flutter his ebony hair. Derek was the perfect Hollywood Lothario—good-looking, a successful filmmaker who drove a sports car and probably had a nice house in the West Los Angeles hills. He'd have his pick of starlets, that was obvious. There was no shortage of girls who'd hop in his bed in hope of furthering their careers.

Yet there was something about him that said he wasn't like that. Or was it simply wishful thinking on her part?

"You don't do the Hollywood social scene, do you, Derek?" she asked when he'd been silent for a while.

He glanced her way. "No, that is, no more than the requirements of the business. A certain amount is done in almost any profession. Even college professors have to schmooze the dean."

"How is it you haven't been seduced?" she asked.

"Probably the same reason you haven't."

"I haven't had the opportunity. I didn't make it as an actress and I'm only getting started as a writer. But you've been in the middle of the action for some time."

Derek stared ahead at the road, not saying anything for a moment. "I take my work seriously and don't want distractions."

"You're hardly a puritan."

He laughed. "No, I like to think I'm just a regular guy. My dad is a college professor, my mom a child psychologist."

"How did you get into films?"

"My girlfriend in high school was an actress and she got me into theater. The acting side didn't appeal, but the behind-the-scenes aspects did. I wrote plays and worked with the director. When I went to U.C.L.A., I decided to major in film arts. I put in my time learning the business, had a couple of lucky breaks. One thing led to another, as they say, and here I am, courting a most promising screenwriter."

Britt chuckled. "Somewhere along the way you learned to flatter."

He took her hand and squeezed it. "Creative people have vivid and lively imaginations, Allison."

He had an easy, natural way of expressing himself, inspiring such confidence and trust that she wanted to throw off her cloak of deception and confess her fraud. His obvious honesty made her feel all the more guilty, the worst being whenever he called her "Allison." Eventually she would tell him the truth, but she couldn't just yet.

For that reason, if for no other, it had probably been a mistake to agree to spend the day with him. She'd simply given in to the temptation of the moment.

"You're passionate about your writing, aren't you?" Derek said.

Britt looked over at him. "Yes. Maybe too passionate. Maybe more possessed and driven than I should be."

"Why do you say that?"

Britt wanted to say, "Because of what I've let it do to me, because of the lie I'm living. And most of all because I'm not true to myself when that should be more important than anything." Instead, she simply said, "Maybe a person can want something too much."

They came to a traffic light and Derek brought the Porsche to a stop. He turned to her. "I've got a hunch this is going to work out fine."

Britt wondered what he meant by that. When he saw the questioning look in her eye, he reached over and pinched her cheek in an affectionate, friendly way.

"All we have to do is trust each other," he said.

The light changed and the car started up. Britt glanced out at the lush green of West L.A., suddenly afraid that by going off with Derek Redmond, she'd made a dreadful mistake.

7

As they drove through Brentwood and Pacific Palisades, Derek chatted about the film he'd just wrapped and the battles at the studio with the publicity department and the way they planned to position the film for the market. Derek was treating her like a colleague and she loved it. For the first time ever, she felt like an insider, someone whose opinion mattered. It was a heady experience.

"I can't wait to see how they try to position *Dream Girl,*" he said. "Unfortunately, the way a film is marketed is nearly as important as the way it's made."

Britt had to remind herself that this was actually her baby they were talking about, not someone else's project. Derek spoke so matter-of-factly. Would the day ever come when she could talk about the success of her work so casually? "I'm sort of curious what they would do myself," she said ironically. "It's hard to imagine that it could really happen."

"First-time nerves?" he asked, understanding her anxiety.

"Yes."

Derek patted her knee. "It'll all be old hat to you soon, Allison. But enjoy it while you can."

"Before I get jaded, you mean?"

"Let's say, before you lose your innocence." He gave her a wink.

When they got to the coast, he turned west and they drove though Topanga Beach and Malibu. They talked about the movie business the whole time. When they got to Corral Beach, he pulled off the highway.

"I guess you aren't exactly dressed for a walk on the beach," he said.

"No."

"If I spring for a new pair of panty hose, will you go for a stroll with me?"

"I suppose I could take them off and spare you the expense."

"Shall I close my eyes?" he asked.

"Why don't you take a little walk instead?"

"Aren't used to getting undressed in a car with a man, huh?"

"I'm a preacher's daughter, Derek. There's got to be at least a pretense of propriety."

"A preacher's kid, eh?"

"I may not seem like it on the surface, but I am and the influences run deep, believe me."

"I won't hold that against you, Allison."

"And I won't hold it against you that you won't," she quipped.

He laughed and climbed out of the Porsche, then strolled off toward the water. Britt watched him looking out to sea as the wind tossed his dark hair. His hands were thrust into his pants pockets. She was more than intrigued by Derek. She liked him. She liked him a lot.

After glancing around the mostly empty parking lot to make sure the coast was clear, she kicked off her shoes, pulled up her skirt and wriggled out of her panty hose. She stuffed them in her purse, then got out of the car. Derek turned when he heard the door slam.

"Are you decent?" he asked, sauntering toward her, a big smile on his face.

"Definitely PG."

Derek chuckled and took her hand. They made their way toward the distant breakers across the broad expanse of sand. It was a pleasant day, but the wind had a nip to it.

"Will you be warm enough?" he asked.

"I'm okay for now, but I may try to talk you out of your jacket later."

"Fair enough."

Britt liked the feel of the sand between her toes. Her big beach experience as a child growing up was at the shore of Lake Michigan. The Pacific was a whole other thing. She had only been to the ocean half-a-dozen times since coming to California, so she could hardly be considered a connoisseur of beach life.

"Don't tell me you were a surfer," Britt said, as they strolled along at water's edge.

"I tried it a few times, but mostly I've sailed."

They talked about their college years. He told her that a turning point in his life had come during the year he'd bummed around Europe following graduation. It was then he'd grown up. In answer to her question, he admitted that there'd been a girl involved in the equation, an English girl who'd been the first serious love of his life.

"So that's what's behind your passion for my screenplay," she observed, tossing her hair in the wind. "An English girl from your past."

"Art reflects life," he said.

"A philosopher, I see."

He laughed. "You know, you're the second person who's said that to me recently. I had lunch with Oliver Wheatley the other day and he said the same thing. Maybe I'm too ponderous. What do you think?"

Britt's ears had pricked up when he mentioned Oliver Wheatley and the rest of what he'd said sailed right over her head. "When was that?"

"When was what?"

"When you had lunch with Oliver Wheatley."

"I don't know, a few days ago," he replied. "Why?"

"I was just curious." Britt was thinking fast, trying to figure out if there was any chance her screenplay or Miranda might have come up in the conversation. She glanced at him, but saw no sign of secret knowledge, no giveaway smile or smirk.

"Oliver's an interesting guy," Derek said as a gust of wind blew hard against them, rippling their clothing. "He was up to his ears in a big film deal when I saw him."

Britt decided there hadn't been anything said that compromised her or the story she'd spun. But it did show she was sailing in very dangerous waters.

"Have you met Oliver?" Derek asked.

She shook her head. "No. You're the first director who's said more to me than 'Thanks for the reading, we'll get back to you.'"

"Directors aren't at their best during casting calls."

"Well, those days are behind me."

"Now you're the genius behind the words, instead of the beauty in front of the camera."

"You keep talking that way, Derek, and I'm going to start believing it. Then I'll become insufferable."

He grinned and put his arm around her shoulders, hugging her. "No, Allison. I can tell you're a lady with her feet firmly on the ground."

They soon came to the end of the beach and turned back toward the car. Britt started getting chilly and asked Derek if he'd be willing to give up his jacket. He promptly slipped it off and put it around her shoulders. She savored the warmth, liking the feeling, the intimacy.

On the way back they watched windsurfers beyond the breakers. Britt waded ankle-deep into the water. The wind was getting stronger, pushing frothy globs of foam across the sand. She clutched the lapels of his jacket together at her throat and skipped ahead.

After a while she stopped and looked back. Derek strolled along unhurriedly, his smile signaling that he was as happy as she. It was nice that they could be like this with each other. Britt almost regretted they had business dealings, that he was the key to getting her writing career off the ground.

"What do you say, Allison, shall we run off to Hawaii?"

"*Hawaii?* I thought you were taking me to *lunch?*"

"Why not both?" he asked, catching up with her.

"You're joking, of course."

He shrugged.

"I think breakfast and lunch is enough for a first date, Derek, but thanks for thinking of me."

He put his arm around her again, intentionally bumping his hip against hers. "I guess I'm just a wild and crazy guy."

"I take it you aren't like this often."

"Not for years, at any rate." He reached over and pulled a strand of windblown hair from her face, smiling. "Maybe it's you."

"Spontaneity is nice and all, but..."

"As a preacher's daughter, you intend to keep me on the straight and narrow—is that what you mean?"

She laughed. "Yes. And get you on the dotted line."

"So that's all you're interested in, eh—selling your script at any cost?" He gave her a bemused smile.

"Not at *any* cost, Derek."

He chuckled. "It's nice to know you've got your limits."

The gentle teasing made her consider her true motives for coming to the beach with him. She *did* want to sell her script; Derek was right about that. After all, that's what had brought them together in the first place. But the truth was, she was enjoying his company, their conversation about the film business. In fact, she liked being with him, period.

"If I didn't know better, I'd say you're blushing," he said, interrupting her thoughts.

Britt gave him a sideward glance. "Must be all the fresh air."

He looked disappointed. "I'd rather think it was me."

She felt a sudden, uncontrollable urge to get away from him, to hide her emotions. On an impulse, she whipped his jacket off and handed it back to him.

"There's something about the seashore that makes me want to run. You don't mind if I jog up the beach, do you?"

"Nope. I love athletic women."

Britt arched a brow. "Maybe you just love women, Derek."

With that she hitched up her skirt and took off at a full run. After a hundred yards she stopped and turned around, her chest heaving. Derek continued walking at the same deliberate pace. She ambled back toward him. Her heart was pounding, but the surge of adrenaline in her blood was spent.

She caught her breath before they met, tossing her hair in the wind. She laughed. "That felt good."

"You're a regular gazelle," he said, peeling off his jacket again and putting it around her. He straightened the shoulders on her slender frame. They stood facing each other. "What other secret talents do you have?"

"You've pretty much seen my repertoire," she replied.

"You weren't Indiana state chess champion?"

"Chinese checkers is my game."

"You were probably Phi Beta Kappa."

"No," she said, "but I did win the seventh-grade spelling bee."

Derek took her face in his hands and looked into her eyes. "I knew you were talented. Now I discover you're an athlete and a scholar to boot. Am I in store for any more surprises?"

Britt shook her head, wishing things had been different. If only she hadn't started this damned charade. It would have been nice to hear the sound of her real name on his lips. "No," she murmured miserably. "What you see is what you get."

"I'd say I got a hell of a bargain." With that he lowered his head and lightly kissed her.

They were frozen in that pose when a wave washed over their feet. Britt jumped from the shock of the cold and Derek looked down at his shoes. They were soaked, as were his socks and pant cuffs.

"Hmm," he said, his hands settling on his hips. "What do you think? We're already wet. Shall we flick it in and go for a swim?"

"Derek, this is a two-hundred-dollar dress! I know that doesn't sound like much to you, but to me it's a whole lot. Anyway, you're the one who's wet. I've got bare feet."

He swooped her into his arms without warning and started walking toward the water.

"Derek! Don't you dare! Put me down!"

"What the hell, I already owe you a pair of panty hose. Why not a new dress?"

Britt tried to wiggle from his arms as another wave came toward them. "If you throw me in the water I'll never speak to you again. And I *won't* sell you my screenplay!"

He stopped dead in his tracks as the wave came swirling up around his ankles, rising to his calves and knees. "You really don't want to go for a swim, do you?"

"I'm impetuous, but not that impetuous."

"Where's your sense of romance? Remember Burt Lancaster and Deborah Kerr in that beach scene in *From Here to Eternity?*"

"They had swimsuits on."

Another wave came in, swirling about his feet. "You're robbing this sparkling moment of its poetry," he lamented wryly.

"I'd rather be dry, thank you."

"Where's your sense of adventure?"

"I left it in your Porsche. Shall we go get it?"

He threw back his head and laughed. "Come on, Allison, tell the truth. In your heart of hearts, what do you want? What is your adventurous spirit crying out for?"

"Lunch."

Shaking his head with amusement, he turned and began trudging out of the surf. "You're a woman who knows her mind."

"That's better than the reverse, isn't it?"

When they got to dry land he put her down. Then he looked at his soaked pant legs. "I either take you to Taco Bell for lunch or we run down to my place so I can change. I'm just down the road a piece."

Britt couldn't help wondering if that was coincidental, or if his spontaneous dip in the Pacific was a ploy to take her to his place. She decided not to make an issue of it. "I'm sure you're not very comfortable, soaked that way."

Derek offered his arm and they marched through the sand back toward the parking lot. "I haven't felt this carefree—or been this silly—in months," he said, "maybe years. Thanks for indulging me."

"I feel pretty good myself, Derek."

He looked up at the clear blue sky. "It's easy enough to understand my euphoria. It's a wonderful fall day. The salt air is invigorating. I'm in the company of a beautiful woman. A new project is spinning around in my head." He gave her a joyful smile. "What's your excuse?"

Britt shrugged. "You like my screenplay and want to turn it into a movie. What could be more exciting to a beginner than that?"

He reached over and gave her a playful cuff on the chin. "You're a tough one, Miss O'Donnell. But I'll do what I can to loosen you up a bit."

"I hope that's not a threat," she said.

Derek grinned. "No, it's a promise."

His place in Brentwood was on a street of stately homes—not magnificent mansions, but substantial residences, many walled and protected by security gates, all opulently landscaped. It was a neighborhood where prominent doctors, lawyers, executives and other well-heeled citizens resided. These were not people who mowed their own lawns.

Britt suspected a few Hollywood types might be scattered about the area, but it wasn't the sort of place tour buses would frequent. They pulled into Derek's circular drive and he stopped.

"You're looking at *Code Red,*" he said. "I was fortunate enough to have a piece of the action."

"Before that you were just one of us, I suppose."

"I had a condo in Santa Monica."

"That still puts you a step above us plebeians."

"Where do you live, Allison?"

"I've got an apartment in West Hollywood. It's musty and furnished in 'early student,' but it's home."

He smiled. "I think I was a previous tenant."

"You were one of Horatio Alger's boys?"

Derek chuckled. "It's nice to be with someone who knows there was life before Edwin Porter and *The Great Train Robbery.*"

"You sound more like an old warhorse than one of Hollywood's young lions, Derek. Next thing you'll be telling me is that you remember the Beatles."

He laughed. "Touché. But you're right, Allison. This town can corrupt a guy. I make a couple of films and I think I know everything."

Britt touched his arm. "That's not what I meant."

"But it's what *I* meant," he said, giving her a wink. "Come on, let's go inside. I'll get out of these wet pants and we'll have lunch."

8

Britt gazed in the guest-bath mirror and had the oddest feeling that the woman who stared back at her was a stranger. All morning she'd been playing Allison O'Donnell, screenwriter. All morning she'd allowed herself to be charmed by Derek Redmond. It had been a crazy, wonderful, exciting day, but a false one. That was the problem.

When she went back out to the sparsely furnished front room there was no sign of Derek. Through the sliding-glass door she could see the pool and the trees and shrubs beyond. The garden had the look of a glade. The living room had two cream leather sofas, an easy chair and a walnut wall-unit. There was an Oriental carpet on the hardwood floor but the decor was clearly of an interim nature. Derek had said he intended to have the place professionally decorated when he could afford it. *Code Red* had been successful, but it hadn't made him a millionaire.

Britt went to the window and watched the pool sweep moving like a robot across the surface of the water. She had to remind herself she was in the home of the director of *Code Red*. Being there seemed too good to be true, and in a way it was, because it was happening under false pretenses.

"Pleasant out there, isn't it?"

Britt turned at the sound of Derek's voice. He was in jeans and a black turtleneck, looking relaxed and much more comfortable than when they'd arrived.

"Yes," she said, "you have a lovely home."

"Why don't we grab a bite? Then, if you like, maybe we can talk about *Dream Girl* a little."

Britt's ears perked up at the mention of her screenplay. Funny that she should have to remind herself that was the point of all this.

Derek took her to the kitchen where they decided on a deli lunch. He kept his refrigerator stocked with meats and cheeses because he wasn't much of a cook and didn't like eating out of a can. Britt offered to help, but he insisted she was his guest.

She watched him bustling about, not exactly looking like he was in his natural environment, but not looking like a fish out of water, either. He was chatting away, making small talk. She responded to his comments, but mostly she was focused on Derek. His casual, natural manner put her at ease. He treated her like a friend, a confidante, which Britt found very disarming. Whenever she found herself relaxing and starting to let her guard down, she had to remind herself where she was and what was going on.

Derek let her take the sandwich fixings to the table while he carried over a couple of different deli salads and two beers. Britt discovered that the ocean air had given her an appetite and she dug in enthusiastically. They munched away contentedly for a while before he spoke.

"*Dream Girl* has a nice, light romantic touch," he said, taking a big bite of his sandwich. "Have you ever been in love the way Casey was in your script?"

Britt considered the question. "Never."

"She's very sympathetic." He took another bite and studied her. "As I get to know you better, Allison, I see her in you."

"Oh?"

"I suppose it's the vulnerability. Her struggle, the fact that she's trying so hard against such formidable odds."

"That's descriptive of my life, too." She took a swig of beer. "Maybe you have a point."

"So, how have the romantic tussles in your life been like Casey's?"

She smiled, giving him a look. "Aren't you the subtle one. I've heard of innovative ways to ask personal questions, but that's the most clever yet."

"That was too personal?"

She nodded. "Maybe."

"Casey is such a fascinating character that it made me curious about you."

"As you well know, Derek, real life is not like fiction." Britt took a bite and chewed. "But I'm glad you liked Casey."

"I fell in love with her, if you want the honest truth." He grinned. "So my curiosity about you is understandable, right?"

She shifted uneasily. "But I'm not Casey."

"Are you sure?"

They looked at each other for a long moment. The tug of energy flowing back and forth between them was strong. Britt knew she was blushing, but she also knew there was no easy way to hide it.

"If I'm embarrassing you, I'm sorry," he said. "I didn't mean to make you uncomfortable."

She wiped the corner of her mouth with one of the paper napkins he'd put on the table. "I've heard of directors getting emotionally caught up with their stars, but I assumed writers were safe from that sort of thing."

"For starters, most screenwriters don't look like you. But that's not the point. It's the soul, the inner spirit revealed in your work, I find myself so attracted to."

She looked into his terribly sincere eyes and couldn't help but be affected by his words, whatever their secret intent. "I don't know what to say, Derek. I'm flattered."

He contemplated her. "Maybe I should confess something else."

Britt's heart skipped a beat. His comments had caught her off guard. She was torn between the joy his flattery brought and her instinct to be cautious.

"When I first saw you," he began, "I wondered if you'd really written *Dream Girl,* or if you were some sort of shill."

Her eyes widened. "A shill?"

"Don't worry, I became convinced you're the real McCoy soon enough. But the idea crossed my mind."

A little wave of trepidation went through her. "Why?"

Derek smiled. "Let's just say you seemed too good to be true." He drank some more beer. "Odd comment from a guy who makes his living by creating illusions, I know."

"I hope you're satisfied now," she ventured.

He nodded. "You're real, all right. Seeing Casey in you is one of the things that convinced me. That and the fact that you know your stuff."

Britt gave a secret sigh of relief.

"It's my job to entertain the public," he said. "But I can't be any better than the material I work with. Therein lies the power of the written word, Allison. If you can make me love Casey, then I can make the people in the movie theaters love her. This magic we work with can be a very powerful thing."

Britt looked at him in awe. Maybe her mouth was even hanging open. She didn't care. She thought she understood her craft, perhaps she even loved it to the point of obsession, but nothing had given her such a sense of pride as the words Derek Redmond had just uttered. "That's a lovely thing to say," she murmured.

"It's from the heart," he said, his eyes shimmering. "And it's a hundred-percent honest. That's important for people who work together, to be completely straight with each other."

A lump formed in her throat. Britt swallowed hard, trying to control her emotion. The euphoria of one moment became the shame of the next. It was all she could do to keep from breaking into tears. The urge to blurt out the truth welled in her again. Her lip trembled.

"It'd be okay to say you feel good about me, too," he prompted.

"Oh, I do! I'm terribly grateful. It's just that I...I..."

"What?"

"Feel so...unworthy."

Derek laughed. "That's a natural rookie reaction. I felt the same way when *Code Red* was finally in the can. I wanted to drive down to the beach and fling all the reels in the ocean. And I might have done it if it weren't for all those investors who'd put millions into it."

Britt bit her lip and a tear actually did overflow her lid. She wiped it away, then dabbed her eye with her napkin. "Thanks for telling me that."

"Hey, I had my mentors, Allison. I hope to be one of yours."

They both smiled and he reached across the table and patted her hand. Britt sighed. She felt tremendous gratitude, but more than that, there was a sense of kinship that was hard to describe.

She recalled one evening while she was in college when she'd had a father-daughter conversation about romance and love. "It's not easy to explain love to somebody who has never felt it," he'd said. "It's the sort of thing a person has to learn about on their own. But I can tell you this, the best is love that's built on friendship, mutual respect, common values and common purpose.''

At the time Thomas Kingsley had said that, the words had sounded an awful lot like the sorts of things he'd said from the pulpit—great-sounding ideas, but not always easy to apply to life. Over the years, though, whenever she was with a guy, she would think about what her father had said. But try as she might, she'd never been able to internalize them—until now, anyway. She'd only met Derek that morning, but he, more than anybody she'd ever known, gave her father's words meaning.

"Assuming you'd allow me, of course," he said.

"Huh?"

"To be your mentor."

Britt gave a little laugh. "Are you kidding? I'd be honored. Who wouldn't be?''

He looked pleased. "Finish your sandwich," he told her. "Then I'd like to show you something.''

Britt insisted on helping to put away the leftovers. Then Derek led her into the front room and sat her down on one of the leather sofas. He went over to a table, got a ringed binder and dropped down beside her so that their hips and shoulders touched. She liked his proximity, his body warmth. Since their walk on the beach she'd craved his touch. She leaned against him.

"What's that?" she asked, gesturing toward the binder resting on his knees.

"*Dream Girl*. I did some work on it last night—until two in the morning, as a matter of fact—and I wanted to share some of my thoughts. If you don't mind."

"Of course, I don't mind."

Derek toyed with the cover of the binder. She squirmed nervously, waiting.

"Don't be alarmed at the extent of my notes and the comments in the margin," he said. "Believe it or not, what I've done is a sign of love."

"That certainly sounds provocative," she said, lifting an eyebrow.

He gave her a crooked grin. "Yeah, it sort of does, doesn't it?"

Britt looked at him from the corner of her eye and he looked at her. *Dream Girl*, the things they'd been discussing, faded and suddenly there was just the two of them. Derek leaned toward her, kissing the end of her nose. Then he kissed her lips.

It seemed so natural, and yet it was surprising in a way. Having him kiss her was what she'd wanted, even if it made no sense.

"I hope you won't always be this distracting," he murmured. "It might be difficult to get anything done."

"*You're* the director."

"In other words, it's my problem," he said with a laugh.

"I guess you could say that."

Derek gave her a chiding look and flipped open the binder. He let it lie open on their laps. "I went through your script line by line, scene by scene. I thought we could walk through it together and do a little fine-tuning."

Britt was thrilled.

For the next two hours they evaluated the script, getting into Casey's head. Derek had diagrammed the plot to look at the structure. Writing, Britt knew from experience, was a lonely business. To delve into it with someone else, to hear another person talking about Casey and her other characters as though they were real, was profoundly moving for her.

Their conversation was animated on occasion, even passionate. A few times Britt got really upset and they snapped at each other. But mostly they were in harmony.

When they finally finished, Derek closed the binder and laid his head back on the sofa, sighing deeply. "I think we just did something very important," he said.

"You think so?"

"Yes. I knew we had to do this together. It's like good sex, when you think about it."

Britt gave him a sideward glance. "I've never quite thought of my writing quite that way."

He laughed and rolled his head toward her. "Maybe it's you, Allison. Maybe you bring it out of me."

Britt leaned away from him. "If you're a pervert, don't try and blame it on me."

Derek turned her face toward him and kissed her again. This was a more passionate kiss. Whatever hesitation or restraint had been there before dropped away and the next thing she knew they were stretched out on the sofa in each other's arms.

Excitement swept over her. Soon they were half undressed, panting, undoing each other's clothes. They rolled off the sofa and onto the floor. Britt landed on top of Derek. She pulled her head back to look at him. There was desire in his eyes. She struggled to catch her breath.

"How did this get into the script?" she asked.

"I think it's been there from the start. We're just discovering it, Allison, that's all."

When he called her Allison, everything suddenly snapped into perspective. She rolled off him and sat up, straightening her dress.

Derek looked perplexed. He propped himself up on his elbow, studying her. "What's the matter?"

"Is this routine?" she asked.

"If you mean do I do this with all my writers, the answer is no."

"Then what happened?"

"I think we're attracted to each other. Or maybe I should say I'm attracted to you."

Britt furrowed her brow. "I'd hate to think this is just a routine step in the filmmaking process."

He laughed. "It's not. If you need an explanation, it's that we share a zeal for our work and for each other. It's actually kind of nice, in my opinion. Both is better." He gave her an inquiring look. "Don't you think?"

She thought for a moment. "So what happens next?"

Derek took her hand. "Well...how about dinner? We can rustle up something here, or I can take you out."

"Derek, we've already eaten breakfast and lunch together. Wouldn't dinner be overdoing it? I mean, I've heard of extended first dates, but this is ridiculous."

"Hell, if I'd had my way, we'd have headed for Hawaii."

"I thought that was a joke."

"I was more serious than not. I admit, though, it wasn't a very practical idea."

Britt shook her head. "You know what? You're crazy."

He shrugged. "Like I told you at the beach, I'm in a spontaneous mood. I don't get this way often, and I thought I ought to go with it." He pulled her hand to his lips and kissed her fingers. "So what will it be, my darling? Dinner in or out, this evening?"

She couldn't help laughing. "You really are crazy."

"Well, what do you want to do?"

"I want you to take me back to the Beverly Hills Hotel so I can get my car and go home."

He frowned, looking unhappy. "Does this mean you're rejecting me?"

"It means I think we should proceed at a slower pace."

"I've been too forward for a first date, is that it?"

"Yes, and for a first picture."

Derek gave her a wink. "Touché." He toyed with her fingers. "Sure I can't convince you to have dinner with me?"

Britt was sorely tempted, but she needed to get her priorities straight. She was here because of her career, not to find romance. That meant she had to get Derek on the dotted line. Unfortunately, that was shaping up to be more difficult than she'd thought. It wasn't easy to say no to him. Reaching out, she touched his face.

"I think we should save something for act two."

"You're definitely a writer, Allison O'Donnell. There's no disputing that!"

9

Britt climbed the stairs to her apartment. She felt totally wrung out. She'd spent a glorious day with Derek. In fact, if she hadn't been under the strain of pretending to be someone she wasn't, it would have been one of the best days of her life. But the guilt she felt over her grand deception just wouldn't go away.

And if that wasn't bad enough, when Derek drove her back to the Beverly Hills Hotel to pick up her car, he'd dropped a bomb. After kissing her sweetly—so sweetly that she'd wished she'd stayed with him—he'd said, "I want you to know I'm going to put the muscle on Miranda, so if you hear about some unhappiness on my part, you won't be surprised."

She'd blinked. "What's the matter?"

"I'm going to insist she meet with me tomorrow. I'm not going to let her put me off again. If she tries to, there'll be fireworks. I wanted you to know in advance so you won't be alarmed."

Britt had thanked him, but the comment had put her into a blue funk. Driving back to her apartment, she'd agonized over what to do. When she got to the third floor Britt went right to Allison's door. Her friend had gotten home a few minutes earlier and was still in her work clothes.

"Britt, what's wrong? You look like you've been hit by a truck."

"I have, Ms. O'Donnell. And in a way you have, too. We've got to talk."

Allison invited her in and Britt went to an easy chair and dropped down in it like a rock. Allison went to the kitchen and returned a moment later with a glass of wine for each of them. Handing one to Britt, she pulled up an ottoman and said, "Okay, what happened?"

Britt gave her a two-minute summary, ending with Derek's intention to have it out with Miranda. "What am I going to do? Not only is my screenplay at stake, but so's my—"

"Future happiness?" Allison said, finishing the sentence for her.

"That might be a little strong."

Allison gave her a skeptical look. "When you were talking about him, I could hear the bells ringing myself. You think you might have found Mr. Wonderful, don't you?"

"Lord, I don't know, Allison. To be honest, I'm so confused I'm not even sure who I am, let alone how I feel about anybody else."

Allison pondered the situation. "Well, you've got yourself a double-barreled problem, kiddo—a professional and a personal one."

"Don't forget you're in this, too. It was your idea."

"*My* idea?"

"Well, *our* idea. Let's not quibble over details." Britt took a slug of wine. "The question is, what am I going to do? Do I turn myself in and cheerfully await execution?"

"Maybe he'd take pity on you."

"Maybe he'd kill me. I would if I was in his shoes. He thinks I'm this wonderful, virtuous, straight-shooting virgin saint."

"Virgin? My, this was quite a first date, wasn't it?"

"Quiet, bitch." Britt sighed woefully. "Seriously, what am I to do? How can I get the deal signed before I do my mea culpa. After everything I've gone through, I can't see giving up at the eleventh hour. On the other hand, Derek's determined. I don't think he'll sign anything without meeting Miranda face-to-face."

"Then maybe he *should* meet with Miranda."

"Are you crazy? If she heard about this, she'd kill me before Derek had a chance."

"I'm not talking about the *real* Miranda. I mean you!"

"Me?"

"You've played her on the phone," Allison said. "Why not play her in person?"

"How am I going to do that? He's already seen me in my Allison O'Donnell role."

"Then you'll have to meet with him in disguise."

"Disguised as what? A bank robber with a ski mask over my face?" Britt took another gulp of wine—a very large one.

Allison was thinking. She had that evil look on her face that Britt had seen before—like when they were hatching her Continental Artists plot.

"I guess I'm somewhat responsible for the pickle you're in," Allison said, "so here's what I'm going to do. I have a friend at the studio, a makeup artist. Lucien owes me a favor anyway, and he's a genius. He'll transform you into a thirty-five-year-old English-woman. Trust me, when Lucien's finished, Derek won't have the slightest idea that Miranda Maxwell and Allison O'Donnell are the same woman."

"You're crazier than I am."

"You don't want to tell him the truth, so what other choice do you have?" Allison asked.

"It's not that I don't *want* to tell him the truth, it's that I *can't.*"

"Don't split hairs, kiddo, we don't have the time. When does he want to meet Miranda?"

"Tomorrow."

"Make it for dinner. That will give us time. I'll have Lucien here after work—say, at six," Allison said. "He'll turn you into Miranda Maxwell for your dinner date. You work out the arrangements with Derek as to the time and place, but you might want to consider someplace dark. What you say and how you handle the negotiation is up to you, Britt. Once I have you in costume, you're on your own."

"Allison, that's the nuttiest idea I've ever heard. It would never work."

"You convinced him you were Miranda over the phone, didn't you?"

"Yes, but..."

"You're trying to tell me Hollywood can turn Dustin Hoffman into Tootsie and Robin Williams into Mrs. Doubtfire, but it can't turn you into Miranda Maxwell?"

"But this is real life!"

"Men never look below the surface, you know that. All Lucien really has to do is make you look unrecognizable, because Derek doesn't know what the real Miranda looks like, does he?"

"No, I guess not. They've never met."

"There you go, then! Piece of cake!"

"Oh, God. I'm going straight to hell. I know I am."

Allison laughed. "It'll be a hell of a trip, though, kiddo."

Britt rolled her eyes. "All right, I guess I'll give it a try. Even if I blow it, I won't be any worse off than I am now."

"Think of it as the role of a lifetime! A final chance to do something with that acting talent of yours."

Allison began laughing. Britt wanted to smack her, but the situation was so absurd that she was soon laughing, too. After a minute they were both practically rolling on the floor.

"The only thing better," Allison said through her tears, "would be if you had to go disguised as a man."

Britt laughed until her sides hurt. Finally she got control of herself. "Glad you're having such a good time with this. I'm the one who's probably going to end up looking like a fool.''

''But if you pull it off, Derek Redmond will have to marry you just to shut you up. He couldn't afford having you running around town telling this story at cocktail parties!''

Britt wiped her eyes. ''And I couldn't afford having him running around town telling the story on me.''

''Guess your mission is clear, Ms. Maxwell. First you get an option agreement signed for your client's screenplay, then you marry the guy.''

''But which one of us is he supposed to marry—you or Miranda or me?''

Allison scratched her head, then a wicked smile crossed her face. ''Know what, kiddo? There may be a movie in this!''

The next day, just before noon, Derek Redmond sat in his black Porsche on Santa Monica Boulevard. He was parked outside the building where Continental Artists was located. Drumming his fingers on the steering wheel, he looked toward the entrance, which was set some distance back from the street. He drew a long breath and stared vacantly through the windshield, curious about what, if anything, Oliver Wheatley would turn up.

Derek was more confused than ever. He'd had a surprising call early that morning from Miranda. The call had actually awakened him.

"Darling, why didn't you tell me you were upset? If I'd known you wanted to meet with me *that* badly, I'd have agreed in a flash. I feel dreadful. You must think me an absolute dollybird. I do hope you'll forgive me. Here I am, trying so hard to be the matchmaker and get you two young people together and I do it all wrong.

"Derek, I promise you on my honor, my sole intent was to let nature take its course, see what would happen when the creative juices started flowing. I wanted you and Allison to feel the match was right. But what happens? I get you all in a rage."

"Miranda, I'm not in a rage," he'd said. "I was concerned because you didn't seem that eager to meet with me to do this deal."

"Nothing could be further from the truth. I miscalculated, that's all. But I've canceled my dinner plans just so that you and I can dine together and discuss *Dream Girl* to your heart's content. I thought perhaps Musso & Frank Grill on Hollywood Boulevard at, say, seven this evening. Would that work for you, love?"

"Sure."

"Oh, and by the way, Allison told me she was terribly impressed with you. She'd previously confided her concern that you might play games with her, but you seem to have allayed her fears in that area. I do hope you're sincere."

"Completely," he'd replied. "I couldn't be more pleased with the way things went yesterday. What I want now is to meet with you and get the deal wrapped up."

"And so we shall, love. Tonight."

"I can't wait."

They'd hung up then. Derek had lain in bed, musing. Miranda—or whoever she really was—had caught him off guard, which was probably her intent. But at least she'd agreed to meet with him, which, he decided, would be interesting if nothing else.

He slept badly, not having fallen asleep until the small hours. All he could think about was Allison. Even *Dream Girl* paled beside his preoccupation with her. In fact, the screenplay seemed almost inconsequential in the greater scheme of things.

He'd teased Allison about whisking her off to Hawaii, but in truth he couldn't think of anything he'd have enjoyed more. It was easy to imagine himself holed up with her in a villa on some isolated, romantic beach. She was one woman he could talk with for a week, a month—maybe a lifetime—without getting bored. He'd never felt that kind of rapport with a woman before. Never.

But the call from Miranda had brought back the issue he'd halfway swept under the carpet. All morning he'd thought about her and Allison, trying to decide what the hell was going on. His best guess was that Allison had hired or cajoled an Englishwoman into posing as Miranda Maxwell. But it had to be either someone with connections at C.A. or someone who actually worked there.

After breakfast he'd given Oliver Wheatley a call to discuss the matter. Oliver had told him he had business at C.A. that morning and would be glad to poke around and see what he could find out. Derek had asked him to be discreet. God knows, he didn't want to upset the applecart before he signed the deal—he badly wanted to make *Dream Girl* his next film. In the end, they decided Derek would drive him to C.A. and they'd do lunch afterward to consider the matter.

Derek glanced toward the building just as Oliver, resplendent in a Harris-tweed sports coat with ascot and matching floppy silk handkerchief, ambled toward the car. He climbed in and sighed.

"Well, old boy, I'm not quite sure what to say. I spoke with Miranda's assistant and got the truth from her. Miranda is in England, I was told, which is what I knew from the beginning. The young lady even had a message for me from her."

"Hmm. Miranda's assistant. Let's see, her name is... Britt, I believe."

"Yes. Miss Kingsley."

"I spoke with her on the phone once or twice. She was the one who initially told me about the script, as a matter of fact." Derek stroked his chin.

"I wonder if you might have spoken with an impostor, Derek. The young lady I spoke with was forthcoming, not the least bit dissembling. Bright and engaging, and most attractive."

"I only spoke with her on the phone so I don't know what she looks like. I was impressed with the way she pitched the script, though. I thought to myself that Miranda had her well trained. It was like she really wanted me to..."

Derek and Oliver looked at each other, the identical thought probably going through their minds.

"You don't suppose this Britt is somehow involved," Derek said.

"An avenue to be pursued, I'd say. Oh, and another point of interest," Oliver went on. "I chatted with Gordon Mallik—he's looking after things for Miranda in her absence."

"And?"

"As you requested, I was discreet. I asked if there were any of my countrymen in the firm, apart from Miranda. The only one was a lad in the mailroom, but I should think he'd be innocent of this involvement."

"Unless he can do a mighty convincing falsetto."

"Quite." Oliver smiled. "I did inquire about your Allison O'Donnell and learned that there's no such person in the firm. The name meant nothing to Gordon."

Derek stroked his chin again, pondering. "You know, I'd have sworn Miranda—the fake one, that is—said something about having gotten the script from one of the other agents at C.A. and it seemed to me she'd said it was Gordon. I remember being struck by the way he'd described it, a Generation X *Bridges of Madison County.*"

"How tantalizing."

"Yes, the whole business is tantalizing. And the plot seems to be thickening."

"Maybe you should go in and have a word with Miss Kingsley yourself. She seems to be the only individual in this melodrama we've been able to put flesh to."

"Yes, but I'm not sure a confrontation is called for at this point."

"Hold on!" the Englishman exclaimed. "There's our young lady now!"

Derek looked toward the building. Two women had come out and were strolling past the fountain on a tangent walkway, headed toward the corner. One was a short plump brunette with a head of unruly dark curls. The other was a beautiful tall blonde—Allison O'Donnell. Derek watched them proceed up the street, his mouth agape.

"I take it you've had some sort of enlightenment," Oliver said ironically.

"You might say so."

"Must I drag it out of you?"

"Oliver," he said, turning to his friend, "the woman I met yesterday...the woman I'm halfway in love with...apparently isn't who she claimed to be."

"Bloody inconvenient. I take it we're talking about Miss Kingsley?"

"Or Allison O'Donnell. I guess it depends on which story you wish to buy."

Oliver shook his head. "I must say, you Yanks have a novel approach to life. Is it the culture or the climate?"

"I don't know. But whatever it is, Hollywood's got it in spades."

They sat musing. "I should think you're going to have a rather interesting dinner engagement with Miranda this evening, Derek."

"You can say that again, Oliver. You can say that again."

10

———◄———

Britt stared at herself in the mirror of Allison's dressing table as Lucien fussed with the dark brown wig. The face she saw looking back at her was no longer hers. She'd been transformed into someone she didn't know.

"This is scary," she said.

Allison, who was standing behind them, her arms folded, had been nursing a big glass of wine throughout the entire operation. "Why scary?" she asked. "Think of it as just another part. The role of your lifetime—if you play your cards right."

"First, I never got that many parts. I was a singularly unsuccessful actress, don't forget. And second, this isn't a play or a film. This is real life."

"Fiddlesticks," Lucien said as he teased a wisp of hair. "Life is just a stage and all the men and women on it actors. Didn't Macbeth or Othello or somebody say that?"

"Right playwright, wrong play."

"Well, I can tell you that with some of the people I work on it's hard to tell whether they're more phony as themselves, or as their characters. In this town, honey, there ain't no real life. That's why nobody lives here anymore but us peons." Lucien was a small, very thin, delicate man of thirty, with an assured manner. "Think of this as Halloween."

"I personally think you look smashing," Allison said, affecting a less-than-convincing British accent.

Britt glanced at the photograph of Miranda she'd brought back with her from the office. She knew Lucien couldn't make her look like the same woman, but she wanted him to capture Miranda's type. The most important thing, though, was that he disguised her well enough so that Derek wouldn't recognize her.

When Allison had hatched this scheme, Britt hadn't thought it would work. But Lucien was a genius. In addition to the dark wig, he'd changed the shape of her nose and the contour of her face, making it appear rounder with thin layers of latex and a careful application of makeup. She also wore false eyelashes and extra-long nails that were painted a pale pink. The final touch to the disguise was a pair of lightly tinted glasses.

When the transformation was complete, Lucien stepped back. Both he and Allison examined Britt carefully. His arms folded, Lucien placed a long thin finger against his cheek. "I wouldn't recognize her as the same person, would you?"

Allison shook her head. "No. You've done a masterful job, Lucien. Really super. She could probably rob a bank and never be identified."

Britt turned around, putting her hands on her hips. "Isn't it enough that you've turned me into a con art-

ist? You want me on the FBI's Most Wanted list now,
too?''

Allison laughed. ''You know what they say, kiddo.
Once you've started a life of crime, there's no turning
back.''

Britt rolled her eyes. ''If my father could only see me
now.''

Britt ended up parking her ancient Toyota in front of
the post office on Wilcox Avenue. Then she walked up
to Hollywood Boulevard, crossed the street, and headed
west toward Musso & Frank Grill. That stretch of the
boulevard had gotten fairly tacky over the years and the
sidewalks were sprinkled with weird-looking characters. Still, the restaurant was a perfect choice, under the
circumstances.

The Grill was the only celebrity hangout Britt had
been in. Six months earlier she and Allison had gone
there for lunch. The two of them had sat at the counter,
eating soup, as they watched the cooks at work. It had
been Allison's treat.

''Every writer should eat where Ernest Hemingway
and F. Scott Fitzgerald used to hang out in the old glory
days of Hollywood,'' she'd said. Their agreement was
that Britt would take her to Musso & Frank when she
sold her first screenplay.

But it was not only her familiarity with the place that
made it desirable. Musso & Frank tended to be dark.
And the darker it was, the better she'd like it.

Nearing the entrance, Britt got increasingly nervous.
She'd been running Miranda's voice through her mind,

but even so, she knew this would be tougher than the telephone act. Derek was a director, used to working with actors—not to mention the fact that he'd gotten to know her as Allison O'Donnell.

God, what if he saw through her act? As she reached for the door handle, she was struck by a crisis of confidence. Had not a group of five or six people come up behind her, virtually pushing her inside, she might have turned on her heel and left. Once in the doorway, she stepped aside to gather herself. Her heart was pounding like crazy. She took a couple of deep breaths, then strode toward the reception desk.

Britt had tried to create a distinctive walk for Miranda, one different from her own. She'd also developed idiosyncratic gestures and mannerisms—some actually borrowed from Miranda, others made up from whole cloth. The idea was to make Britt's two personas as distinctive and unalike as possible.

She was wearing a dark gray gabardine suit she'd borrowed from Allison and a plain white silk blouse. The suit was well made and expensive, but a little out of style. The skirt was long on her. The effect bordered on frumpy, but not overly so. Miranda was understated in her dress and certainly not stylish. Britt had approximated the look.

The heavyset maître d' was on the phone, probably taking a reservation, as she waited. Britt was running Miranda's persona through her mind when she suddenly wondered if she'd remembered to stick the option agreement form Sally Farland had given her into her purse. Rummaging through her bag, she was re-

lieved to discover the contract was there. Britt sighed.
She intended to get Derek Redmond on the dotted line
that evening. God knew, she wouldn't go through this
again.

"Yes, ma'am?" the maître d' said.

Britt looked up at him as another crisis of confidence struck. "I'm . . . meeting someone," she stammered. "Derek Redmond."

"Oh, yes. Mr. Redmond is expecting you. I'll show
you to his table. This way, please."

They made their way into the huge dining room that
hadn't been redecorated since the 1930s. Hardly anyone glanced her way, but Britt felt that her every step
was under scrutiny.

They went to the far corner. Britt couldn't see past the
maître d', but when they arrived at the table, she found
herself face-to-face with Derek. He was in a charcoal
gray sport coat and black turtleneck and looked dev-
astatingly handsome. Seeing him, she froze. Her mouth
went dry. A lump formed in her throat. She felt nau-
seous and even thought for a moment she might faint.

Derek had an expectant look on his face, but there
was no telltale sign of recognition, thank God. He got
to his feet.

"Miranda," he said warmly, as he stepped around the
table, extending his hand, "how good to meet you at
last."

Britt gave him a brittle smile. "It is so lovely to be
here," she chirped, mercifully falling right into the role.
"I'm delighted."

He pressed his cheek to hers and Britt stiffened, sure that the latex on her face would shift, or her nose would crack. But it didn't. Derek smiled pleasantly, so she assumed she was still intact.

"You seem to have forgiven me," she said, looking up into his clear green eyes.

"I'm relieved that we've finally gotten together," he replied, helping her with her chair. "Let me put it that way."

He returned to his place. They gazed at each other. She was glad the dining room was relatively dark. Still, she could see him clearly, which meant that he could see her. Of course, he wouldn't be suspecting anything and that was in her favor. Britt tried her best to be nonchalant as she favored him with a little smile.

"So," she began, "you're taken with both my client and her work."

"'Taken' is a real understatement, Miranda," he said. "The screenplay is terrific and I love Allison. She's a wonderful, wonderful person."

He smiled into her eyes and Britt felt herself flush under the latex mask. "Then I guess there's nothing left but to do the paperwork at this point," she said decisively.

He picked up his water glass and took a sip. "Well, that and to celebrate," he added. "I thought it might be nice if the three of got together to toast the success of *Dream Girl.*"

"That would be lovely, Derek. Let's plan on it sometime in the future. On the weekend, perhaps."

"Why put it off? In fact, I thought I might ask Oliver to join us. After all, if he hadn't thought so highly of you in the first place, I never would have given your office a call, and I'd never have heard about *Dream Girl*."

"Yes, well . . . bloody fortunate, that."

"And you know what," Derek continued, "while we're at it, we really ought to include your assistant, Britt. I mean, she's the one responsible for us all getting together. Besides, Oliver tells me she's quite a charming young lady. Attractive, too."

"Yes, well, Britt has her moments, I must say. But I don't know that she'd be all that interested."

Derek grinned. "Been in Hollywood so long she's become jaded, eh? Seen one director, seen 'em all."

"Well, no, certainly not that. . . . It's just that—"

"Tell her for me I'd like very much to meet her and express my personal thanks."

Britt swallowed hard. "I shall, Derek. I'm sure she'd be pleased."

The waiter came to take their drink orders. Britt was thankful for the respite. She ordered a vodka martini—something she never did. Usually the extent of her drinking was a glass of wine or two, but tonight she felt she needed all the help she could get.

She watched Derek as he spoke with the waiter, admiring his cool, confident manner. Of course, *he* wasn't playing a role. It was easy for him. She, on the other hand, was a nervous wreck. She was sweating profusely and was scared to death that the latex would start to slide off her face.

"So, you've spoken to Allison," he said when the waiter had gone off to fill their drink order, "and she's pleased with the way things are going?"

"Positively delighted. Allison feels a real rapport with you. Creatively speaking, I mean."

"Only creatively?"

Britt blushed deeply and for the first time that night was glad to have the mask and all the makeup on. "She seemed to find you charming. Let me put it that way."

"I find her charming, as well," he said. "I like her a lot, in fact. Maybe too much."

Britt smothered a self-satisfied grin. "Too much? How so?"

"Well, you know how distracting personal attraction can be in a professional relationship." He fiddled with the silverware on the table. "Tell me, Miranda, do you think it would be a mistake for me to get involved with her?"

Britt swallowed hard. "Well...do you want to get involved with her?"

"I was taken by her. She certainly seemed interested in me, too. But in the back of my mind I couldn't help...wondering."

"Wondering what?"

"If her...friendliness, shall we say...was calculated to get me on the dotted line."

"I'm sure not, Derek. I don't know Allison awfully well, mind, but I think she's perfectly sincere. Don't forget, you'd decided you liked her screenplay before you'd even laid eyes on her."

"Yes, that's true. But the price hasn't been agreed upon yet. And there's the future to consider. Maybe I'm paranoid, Miranda, but a guy always wonders when a woman comes on to him that way."

Britt bristled. "I . . . You mean, *she* came on to you? You're saying she was the one—"

Derek was looking off, reflecting. Britt was livid. What a pompous, hypocritical bastard he was! What did he mean, *she* had come on to him? *He'd* tried to seduce *her!* And he'd seemed like such a gentleman when they were together.

"It could be she misunderstood me," he said thoughtfully.

"And it could be you misunderstood *her*, love. How do you know Allison's feelings for you aren't entirely professional? Perhaps you misconstrued her enthusiasm for the project as enthusiasm for you!"

Derek considered that. "Now that would be unfortunate, wouldn't it? I sort of enjoyed the flattery of thinking it was me who interested her most."

Britt had all she could do to keep from leaning across the table and slapping his face. She clenched her fists, hating the man's arrogance.

Their drinks arrived and Britt lost no time in picking up her glass. She would have taken a slug immediately if Derek hadn't extended his own glass, proffering a toast.

"To you, Miranda, who made this possible. To *Dream Girl*, the next big romantic-comedy hit, and to Allison O'Donnell, the creative genius behind it all."

Britt took a healthy gulp. "I'm surprised you'd want to drink to her," she said, sounding more miffed than she'd intended.

"Oh, but of course I want to drink to her. I love Allison. Her mind, her talent, her beauty, her body—you name it."

"Really? A minute ago you practically said she was a conniving opportunist." Her eyes narrowed and she gave him a long, penetrating look. "Or did I misconstrue your remarks?"

"No, that isn't what I meant at all. I was simply concerned that her feelings for me weren't genuine, that doing the deal was more important than... well, the relationship."

"She might wonder the same thing about you, mightn't she?"

He fiddled with his drink glass as he considered that. "I certainly hope that's not the case. I was completely taken with her, but..."

"But what?"

"Underneath I sensed something was wrong—not quite... how shall I put it? Not what it was represented to be. Naturally I wondered if she was deceiving me. If maybe her feelings weren't genuine."

"I should think that would become obvious one way or the other in time. A person can't be ingenuine forever—if they are at all," she finished, clearing her throat.

He gave her a wry smile. "So I should go ahead with the deal and see what happens? Is that what you're saying? Forgive me, Miranda, but that sounds like an agent talking to me. This is not just another picture, it's my professional and personal life we're talking about."

Britt sighed with exasperation. "Why don't you just tell me what it is you want, then?"

"I want to do *Dream Girl* and I want an honest, sincere and—shall we say, meaningful?—relationship with Allison O'Donnell."

Britt reached down and took her purse. "That's what I want, Derek, and I believe it's what Allison wants." She removed the option agreement she'd drawn up that afternoon with Sally's help and handed it to him. "I think the time has come to stop talking and be done with it. Once we've signed this, everything will fall into place, I'm sure."

Derek looked at the paper and Britt picked up her glass, taking another healthy gulp of the martini. She watched him reading the agreement.

"You've left the price blank," he said.

"I discussed it with Allison, and she and I are of the mind that you should propose a figure based on your feelings about the project."

"My feelings about the project or my feelings about her?"

"The project, Derek."

He looked at the contract again. "You've left off the names of the parties, too, I see. Is that an oversight?"

Britt's stomach tightened. She knew she'd have to finesse the author's name because she couldn't write in Allison O'Donnell when Britt Kingsley was legally the contracting party. "I wasn't sure if you did your deals individually or if you have a production company," she ventured.

"I option projects in my own name," he replied.

"Then you can enter your name, darling. I'll fill in the author's portion when I get Allison's signature.

"I see," Derek said.

Britt took a pen from her purse. "So, what figure shall we put in?"

Derek stroked his chin. "It's her first screenplay, so Guild minimum plus, say, twenty-five percent is fair, don't you think?"

Britt was thrilled. That was a lot of money. Of course, Derek would have to get financing before he exercised the option, but it was a start. A good start. And somehow she was certain they'd make the picture.

It was all she could do to keep from bouncing in her chair, but she knew she had to hold herself together until everything was properly signed. She took a calming breath and looked Derek in the eye. "I'm sure that would be acceptable. What about the option price?"

Derek studied her. Britt felt the perspiration running down her back.

"How about twenty-five thousand?" he prompted.

"Agreed."

"Shall I write the figure in?"

Britt handed him the pen and watched him fill in the blanks. Her heart was racing and once again she felt light-headed. But she reached down inside herself, summoning her willpower. Just a bit longer, and she could get out of there.

"Go ahead and sign it, love," she said jauntily. "Once I've gotten Allison's signature, I'll have the agreement delivered to you. On receipt of your copy you can issue the check."

Sally had explained the procedure to her, so she spoke with some assurance on the point. Derek's pen moved to the bottom of the page, where it hovered. After a short hesitation, he looked up at her.

"You know, this is a big moment for Allison. I really think she ought to be present so she can enjoy it with us. It would be nice if we both signed at the same time. Why don't I give her a buzz and see if she can come over here?"

Britt's heart practically stopped as Derek reached down, got his briefcase and removed his cellular phone. "Can you tell me her number?"

"Well . . . uh, do you really think this is necessary? I mean, it would be jolly fun, but Allison is not anticipating—"

"Oh, come, Miranda. Her first film deal. Of course, she'd want to be here. She lives in West Hollywood, so she could probably get here in twenty minutes."

The knot in Britt's stomach was so big that she wondered if she might get sick. Hold on! she told herself. You've come this far!

Her mind spinning, Britt reached for Derek's phone, taking it from his hand. "Here, love, let me ring her up and see if she can drop by for the ceremony."

Britt forced a tight smile, but she was furious with Derek for putting her through this. But she told herself that he could not have done it intentionally. He undoubtedly thought Allison would be thrilled.

Britt dialed Allison's number, figuring she could alert her friend to what was happening and maybe get some help in the process. Allison answered after a couple of rings.

"Allison, dear, Miranda here. Derek and I are having a delightful meeting. We've negotiated all the messy details, but Derek, being the dear, thoughtful boy he is, suggested you come by and have a drink with us while we sign. Can you pop into Musso & Frank Grill and finalize the contract with us?"

"Britt, you're in trouble, aren't you?" Allison replied.

"Not really, love. We just want your participation."

"You need a suggestion," Allison said, sounding every bit as panicky as Britt was feeling.

"That would be lovely, dear—if you can figure a way," Britt said, smiling at Derek.

"Put him off," Allison said. "Tell him I'm—I mean, you're . . . sick or something."

"But darling, this must be done tonight. We've all waited long enough. Poor, dear Derek is so eager to get this done and I know you are, as well. Can't you find a way?"

"Uh . . . uh . . . tell him I—I mean you—will meet him later. Then you can sign the contract after you've gotten out of your Miranda costume."

"Capital idea! I'll arrange it." Britt punched the Off button and handed the phone back to Derek.

"Is she coming?"

"She is indisposed, and it would be a hour or more at best before she could make it down here. But she shares your enthusiasm for signing this evening. She proposed she'd drive by your place in two hours' time so you can do the honors there. Surely that would do, wouldn't it?"

Derek rolled the question through his mind. "I guess that would work. We can drive over after we've finished dinner and wait for Allison."

"I'd love to, honestly. But I've got a rendezvous of my own later this evening," she said, flickering her eyebrow. "If you know what I mean, darling."

"Ah, yes, of course, Miranda." He folded up the contract and stuck it in his jacket pocket, then handed Britt back her pen.

She watched, realizing he had the option agreement and it was still unsigned. Britt suddenly hated her life and every lie she'd ever told, especially those of the past several days. God was getting even with her, she was certain.

"Well," Derek said, signaling the waiter, "we might as well go ahead and have dinner. How about another drink while we wait for our meals?"

Britt looked at her mostly empty glass. She had the good sense not to accept the offer, knowing that after another drink she'd be speaking English with a Polish accent. "Thank you, darling, but I'll decline," she said. "In fact, I'm considering doing something horribly impolite. I'm thinking about begging off dinner and asking you if sharing a drink as we have won't be sufficient for our first meeting."

"You want to leave?"

"The gentleman I'm seeing later is very special and...well, what truly matters is you and Allison." She gave him a broad smile. "I've done my part by setting the wheel of fate in motion. Won't you allow me to bow out?"

Derek reached over and patted her hand. "If that's what you want, Miranda."

"Smashing!" she said. "I'll take my leave of you, then. It has been oh-so-delightful, Derek. It positively has."

She got up and so did he. Britt gave him a quick peck on the cheek. "Give my love to Allison, darling. And by all means don't give the girl a hard time. Ta-ta!" she said with a smile, then turned and walked from the room. It took all the restraint she had to keep from running, but she made it out of the dining room and to the entrance without incident. A moment later she was outside, sprinting up the street, headed for home.

11

Britt paced back and forth in her bedroom as Allison sat watching her. She was wearing her bathrobe now and she was livid.

"Damn him, anyway," she said. "Derek had the pen in his hand, the contract was lying right in front of him, and he didn't sign it. I could have killed him!"

"He was just thinking of you, Britt—I mean, you in the guise of me."

"Well, then, I wish he wasn't so damn considerate." Allison laughed.

"It's not funny," Britt insisted. "It's tragic. I can't tell you how much I want this behind me."

"But even after it's finished, you'll have the problem of explaining who you really are."

"Yes, but I'll have my deal. And if Derek or Miranda or both of them want to kill me at that point, at least I won't have to die in vain. The worst would be if I lost the deal, Derek's friendship and respect, and got fired by Miranda, to boot—all of which seems to be getting more probable by the hour."

"Not necessarily," Allison said. "Derek still doesn't know what's going on. He's got the contract in his pocket and all you need to do is go to his place, bat your eyelashes a little, get his signature, and come home."

"Granted, it sounds simple, but I've learned from experience that nothing works like it's supposed to. Each step I've taken was supposed to be the last, and each time it's ended up leading to another one. This is like one of those nightmares about being chased—you don't get caught, but you can't escape, either."

"At least you still have a chance to pull it off."

"Yeah, but only because I've become the biggest fraud in Hollywood."

"An hour or so from now it will be over," Allison reminded. "Hang in there."

Britt dropped down on the bed and sighed. Allison went over and sat next to her, putting her arms around her shoulders.

"You know," Britt said, "the worst part is I'm not even sure what I want anymore. I really do care about Derek and that makes everything especially painful. If it wasn't for my damned screenplay I'd be on the beach with him in Hawaii right now."

"If it wasn't for your damned screenplay, you'd never even have met him."

Britt chuckled, shaking her head. "The classic case of good news, bad news."

"So what are you going to do?"

"Finish what I started, I guess. I've gone through hell, the past few days. I can't quit now, Allison."

"I know how important *Dream Girl* is to you."

It *was* important. To give up now would be tantamount to discounting everything she'd gone through over the past few years. How could she turn her back on it when victory was within her grasp? The problem was she had a lot of guilt, which made the prospect of getting caught with her hand in the cookie jar so painful.

Britt looked at her watch. "Well, I'd better drive over to Derek's and get this over with."

She went to her closet and got out a pair of freshly pressed jeans. Then she got the fisherman's-knit sweater her father had given her for Christmas from her chest of drawers. Allison watched her.

"Regardless of how things turn out," she said, "I want you to know I admire you for your guts. There aren't many people who could do what you've done."

"There aren't many people this stupid," Britt answered ruefully.

Allison gave her a big hug. "Having fire in the belly is worth a lot in this town. People respect determination. I know it'll work out." She went to the door, where she stopped. "It's the last act, kiddo. Break a leg."

Britt nodded. "I'll do my best."

Derek poured himself a glass of orange juice, then strolled through the house, drinking it. He checked his watch as he went into the front room. Allison—Britt, that is—was due at any time. He hardly knew what to expect.

Miranda—or whoever the hell the woman at Musso & Frank's was—had left the restaurant so abruptly he hadn't had time to react. He found that behavior strange. In fact, he'd found the woman herself strange, a difficult person to peg.

On the whole she was credible, although he'd detected a minor lapse in her accent—enough to suggest that she might not even be a Brit. He'd rather liked her, though. She was quirky and a hell of a con.

Truth be known, he found the hoax and everybody involved in it rather amusing. What a charming band of hustlers he'd gotten tied up with—Allison/Britt and the putative Miranda. It would make a good movie—something worth keeping in mind.

Derek stared out the sliding-glass door at the brightly lit pool, gleaming in the darkness of his backyard. He took a long drink and wondered what sort of line Britt would give him this time. He couldn't decide whether he should confront her or not. He was inclined to play along with her game, if only to see what she was going to do next.

Just then Derek heard a car outside. He finished his juice, took the glass to the kitchen and headed for the front door. The doorbell rang as he reached the entry hall.

Opening the door he found her on the porch. She was wearing tight jeans and a bulky, white fisherman's-knit sweater. She'd slung a black leather purse over her shoulder. She looked so inviting—wholesome and well scrubbed—not at all like the sophisticated woman he'd met at the Polo Lounge. This, he judged, was the down-to-earth side of Allison—or Britt. The girl from a small town in Indiana. The innocent.

"Good evening, Allison," he said, giving her a welcoming smile.

"Hi."

"Come on in."

She stepped inside. He closed the door and they stood looking at each other.

"Thanks for coming over," he said.

"Thanks for inviting me. Miranda told me you thought I should be present for the signing of the contract since it's such a big occasion for me. That was very thoughtful of you."

He shrugged. "It was an excuse as much as anything else."

"An excuse for what?"

"For seeing you, being able to share the moment."

She gave him a faint smile. "You're a romantic, aren't you, Derek?"

"You gotta have feelings of some kind to make films, especially relationship films."

She seemed uncomfortable, more circumspect than he'd have expected, given the way things had gone between them last time. He leaned against the door, appraising her.

"I hope I didn't tear you away from anything important."

"Oh, no, I . . . was just having dinner with someone, a friend. He understood."

Derek was a little taken aback. "Oh. I'm sorry. I didn't realize. I mean, Miranda didn't say anything." He felt a pang of jealousy, something he wasn't accustomed to. "Had I known, I wouldn't have insisted that—"

"No, it's all right," she said. "Really."

"You're sure?"

"Honest. I wouldn't have missed this for anything."

He was glad she'd said that. God knows, he wanted it to be true. But the fact remained that she'd deceived him once already by assuming a false identity. That sort of made him question her feelings now. About the only thing Derek was absolutely certain of was that she was the author of *Dream Girl*.

He stepped over and took her hands. She gave him her first real smile and he embraced her. When she was in his arms, he felt the oddest desire. He wanted to say, "Look, I know you're a phony. But it doesn't matter. I don't care because I like you just the way you are." But try as he might, he couldn't get the words out.

So he stood there silently, holding her, inhaling her clean, fresh scent as he stroked her head. He had another desire then....

"Why do I like this so much?" he asked, running his hand through the silky hair at the back of her neck.

She looked up at him. "Do you?"

He noticed there were tears running down her cheeks and he was surprised. "Allison, what's the matter?"

She half laughed through her tears. "I guess I'm feeling emotional."

"*Happy* emotional?"

She wiped her face with her sleeve and nodded. It wasn't a very convincing response.

"You must cry all the time at weddings," he said, giving her his handkerchief.

Britt dabbed her eyes and gave it back to him. "Not really. I don't know what overcame me. I'm sorry."

"No need to apologize," he replied. "I'm ready to cry myself."

She gave him a skeptical look. "Because you're happy?"

He shrugged. "Because you are."

She searched his eyes and the tears welled again. "Give me that handkerchief back," she mumbled.

He did. She wiped her eyes again. Then he led her toward the front room. "I think it's time we put on our happy faces," he said. "After all, this *is* a celebration." When they entered the room, he gestured toward the stereo system. "Why don't you pick out some music, whatever meets your fancy, and I'll get the champagne?"

"Champagne?"

"We're celebrating, aren't we?" He gave her a wink and headed for the kitchen, feeling as emotional as she.

Britt flipped through the CDs, hardly seeing the discs. Instead, she was thinking about Derek, how sweet he was being. Her annoyance for him having put her through an ordeal at the restaurant had dissipated—after all, there was no way he could have known the consequences of what he was putting her through, so it was hardly fair to blame him for that. And if he'd bent the truth when he'd told Miranda that *she'd* come on to *him* the day before, instead of the other way around, well, his white lie was nothing compared to her black ones!

On the drive over, Britt had decided to make the evening short and sweet. Now that she was here, she felt sentimental; she no longer wanted to pressure Derek into signing just so that she could get her confession out of the way. She'd let him sign the contract at his own pace.

She heard the pop of a champagne cork in the other room. Moments later Derek returned with an ice bucket, a bottle of champagne and two flutes. He put everything on the end table next to the sofa.

"Find something you like?" he asked.

Britt hadn't paid much attention to what she was looking at, except to note that most of the recordings were jazz piano. "These all look good. Who's your favorite?"

"I like both George Shearing and Marian McPartland," he replied, taking the bottle from the ice bucket. "I have several recordings by each of them."

Britt snatched a couple of compact discs from the tray. "I'll let you put them on."

Derek finished pouring some champagne into each of their flutes and carried them to the stereo, where she was waiting. He handed Britt one. "To *Dream Girl,*" he said, gazing into her eyes. "And to us. May we have a long and fruitful collaboration. I hope this is only the beginning."

Britt's eyes filled. She was making a habit of wearing her emotions on her sleeve. Derek could hardly say a thing without her getting misty.

She blinked back her tears. "Thank you for appreciating my work," she said softly.

They touched glasses and each took a sip. Britt watched as he set down his flute and put the CDs on. It was hard for her to accept that it had only been twenty-four hours since she'd first come to this house—it seemed like she'd known Derek for weeks, if not months. That old cliché about meeting someone and feeling as if you'd known them forever now made sense. She'd gone out with some guys half-a-dozen times or more, and still hadn't had a clear idea what they were like as human beings.

Derek was different. He wasn't afraid to expose his vulnerabilities. Artists, she'd learned, often did that. They had to risk themselves if they wanted to reach their audience in a profound way. This was true of filmmaking and writing, both. They had that in common.

"So, what are you thinking?" he asked.

"You heard the wheels turning, huh?"

"It was making a terrible racket," he teased.

Britt leaned back, reflecting. "I guess I'm savoring the moment. Enjoying the chance to relax."

In truth, now that she'd let herself slow down for the first time in hours, she realized that she felt spent, just like she had after a tough performance back in her old acting days. God knows, that night, as Miranda Maxwell, she'd given one of her most demanding performances ever, although she could hardly claim it as one of her prouder moments.

When she thought about it, though, she was still acting. She had to be Allison for a little bit longer. But at least she was out of costume and able to be herself in all but name. For that, she was grateful. She hungered to be honest—dead honest—more than anything.

"The day I signed on to direct my first picture I was bouncing off the walls," he said. "I guess we each deal with our triumphs in our own unique way."

"I'm having trouble putting it all in perspective, if you want to know the truth," she told him.

Derek, who was sitting close to her, took her hand. "The important thing is that you're happy."

Britt leaned against him, liking the feel of his body. "You've been very good to me. I'd like to..."

"To what, Allison?"

"I don't know. Feel more deserving, maybe."

"Don't be silly. Relax and enjoy yourself."

Britt wished she could. She wished it more than anything in the world. But it wouldn't happen—not until this lie she was living was behind her.

They drank champagne and talked about *Dream Girl*. She liked it when they discussed their work. Ironically, it was at these moments that she was most herself, and felt closest to Derek.

Soon, between the chanpagne and Derek's comfortable manner, she felt mellow. By the time he'd drained the last of the champagne into her glass, she was starting to enjoy herself.

Derek had been toying with her hair. As they talked, he'd kissed her temple a time or two. Each time she'd felt his warm breath on her ear, she'd shivered, but she'd managed to keep the conversation rolling anyway. Now the talk about their work sort of faded and her awareness of him took center stage.

Her inhibitions gone, Britt had no trouble following her desires. She put her hand on Derek's thigh, even knowing it was forward, a suggestive thing to do. It was Dutch courage, but it was working.

Britt was conscious of the lean firmness of his leg. She gave it a little squeeze. "You know what, Mr. Redmond?" she said.

"What, Miss O'Donnell?"

Britt shivered, coming very close to telling him that wasn't her name and she didn't want to be called Allison O'Donnell anymore. "It's occurred to me that we're celebrating and we still haven't signed the contract."

He gave her an ornery smile. "You noticed."

"I noticed."

He stroked her cheek with his finger. "But if we don't sign it now, then we'll have an excuse to celebrate again tomorrow—when we do sign."

"Tomorrow?"

Derek shrugged. "Why not?"

"Why wait?"

He pushed a strand of hair off her temple and leaned close. "There's nice soft jazz on the stereo, I'm feeling good, and I've got the most beautiful screenwriter in North America and maybe the world, right here beside me. A contract's the furthest thing from my mind."

Britt sat up straight and pulled away from him. What did he mean? That he wanted her to come over here to seduce her, not because he was serious about a deal?

"Allison," he said, drawing her back into his embrace, "is something wrong?"

She looked him in the eye. "I'm not sure where I stand, all of a sudden. Are you saying the deal isn't important to you but seducing me is?"

"*Am* I seducing you?" he asked.

She sighed. "You aren't playing tiddledywinks, Derek."

"Would you rather I sit across the room?" he asked. But as he spoke, the tip of his index finger moved lightly over her cheekbone.

She gave him a look. "Dirty pool."

"Better than tiddledywinks," he said with a laugh.

She took his hand and put it on his lap. Then she folded her arms over her chest. "I'm not going to bed with you to get you to sign that contract."

"Did I say that's what I wanted?"

"I feel it's implied."

"I certainly wouldn't want you thinking that. I'll get the contract now," he said matter-of-factly. "Then we won't have to discuss it anymore."

He got up and left the room. Britt pondered the situation. She'd resolved not to press him about the contract, but she had not felt right about the way things were going. Her chain of lies was the problem. But until Derek signed the agreement and she told him the truth, she'd have to live with the consequences of her actions.

Derek returned. He had a pen in his hand and the form that she'd given him earlier that evening. After plopping down on the sofa, he leaned forward and put the contract on the coffee table. He took the pen, filled in his name in the appropriate place and signed. Then he handed her the contract and the pen. "There you are, my dear. You've got me on the dotted line. You can sign and leave if that's what you wish."

Britt looked at the form. This was what she'd been working for. This was what she'd all but sold her soul to the devil to have. She stared at the blank space where she had to insert her name. All she had to do was write in "Britt Kingsley" and tell him what she'd done. She didn't even have to go into any detail if she didn't want to.

"What's the matter?" Derek asked, when she'd sat for a minute without moving.

Britt put the form down on the coffee table. "Thank you for signing that, Derek. I'm sorry I doubted your motives."

"Aren't you going to sign it?"

"Yes. Later." She took his hand and looked into his clear green eyes. "But there's some nice jazz playing, I'm feeling good and I've got the most dashing film director in North America and maybe the world, right here beside me. The contract's the last thing on my mind right now."

Derek smiled. "You're one crazy lady. Has anyone ever told you that?"

"Not quite so romantically."

Smiling, he leaned over and kissed her. Britt put her arms around his neck and they fell back on his sofa. Soon they were kissing passionately. She wanted him.

She wanted him badly. Right then, he was all she cared about, all that mattered.

Within moments Derek was pulling off her sweater and she was unbuttoning his shirt. Her jeans went flying, then her bra. Britt sat astride him, looking into his eyes. She put her hands on the dark mat of hair on his chest as he caressed the tips of her nipples with his thumbs.

She moaned. If it felt like she'd known him forever, it also seemed like she'd wanted him forever, too. He pulled her down on top of him, crushing her against his chest, taking her mouth and kissing her deeply.

Her head was spinning. She couldn't tell how much of it was the champagne, and how much was the dizzy excitement of his kiss. After a while she pulled back to catch her breath and stare into his eyes.

"I understand now where Casey got her fire," he mumbled.

"Is this why you loved her?"

"It's *how* I would have loved her."

"I'm not my character, Derek."

"And this is not a movie." He kissed her again.

Derek was holding her, stroking her head. She felt the pounding of her heart. He gazed into her eyes. Britt knew it was time.

"Shall I carry you to the bedroom?" he whispered.

"Men actually do that in real life?"

He smiled as George Shearing's piano music tinkled softly in the background. "They do in Hollywood, my darling."

12

Britt awoke early. The sun was up and the soft morning air was coming in the partly open sliding-glass door of Derek's bedroom. He was sleeping peacefully.

Britt smiled, recalling how wonderful it had been, making love with Derek. After he'd carried her to the bedroom, they had slowed down, each of them wanting to savor the experience, drag it out. When Derek had put her on the bed he'd said that there could only be one first time for them, and he wanted to make it last.

He'd seduced her slowly, kissing her everywhere, making her tremble with desire. The sheets had felt cool when he'd laid her on the bed, but soon her skin was hot. She felt warm and creamy, ready. And yet, she didn't mind waiting. The anticipation was sweet.

Derek had taken his time, licking and kissing her from her toes and ankles to her upper thighs. He ran his tongue up the inside of each leg. His tongue felt hot, but when the balmy air flowing in the sliding-glass door hit the moist patches of her skin, Britt shivered. It was incredibly erotic.

Best of all was when he'd stopped the teasing and parted her curls to kiss her center. Britt inched closer to him and clutched the sheets in her fists as he stroked her. The joy was exquisite and for a moment she thought she would come that way. But Derek pulled back, apparently sensing she was on the edge.

By the time he'd finally entered her, she was more than ready. Never had sex been so fulfilling. Holding her afterward, he'd whispered that he never used the word *love* lightly, but his feelings for her were special. He'd never gone to bed with one of his actresses—and certainly not one of his screenwriters—but it seemed entirely natural to be making love with her.

Britt had cried after he'd said that. He'd asked her what was wrong and she'd almost told him the truth. But she didn't want the evening to end with a tearful confession. If this was to be their one and only time together, she wanted it to be perfect. Morning would come soon enough. She would tell him then.

They'd made love one more time in the middle of the night. For Britt it had been bittersweet, in part because she was less carried away by the passion of the moment. She desired him—wanted to be a part of him—but she'd had time to put things into perspective. She could no longer pretend that she could avoid facing up to reality.

Now it was time for her mea culpa.

Britt looked over at Derek, hoping he wouldn't hate her afterward. Even if he was angry with her, perhaps in time he would forgive her.

She crawled out of bed and headed for the shower. When she'd finished dressing, she returned to the bedroom. Derek was still asleep. Not wanting to awaken him, she padded off to the kitchen and got some orange juice. Then she went to the front room and found the contract where they'd left it.

Taking the pen, she filled in her real name and signed at the bottom, next to Derek's signature. She'd already decided that was how she'd tell him. She would show him the form and explain why she'd signed as Britt Kingsley instead of Allison O'Donnell. And then, if he didn't strangle her on the spot, she would tell him the whole sordid tale.

The pool was beautiful in the morning sun. Britt picked up her glass of juice and the contract, opened the sliding-glass door, and then stepped onto the patio. Although it was early, the air temperature was pleasant. She strolled over to the pool and sat down at the umbrella table at the far end. She would drink her juice and enjoy the setting while waiting for Derek to awaken.

There were some beautiful flowering shrubs around her. Birds were singing in the trees. Britt watched a calico cat slink along a fence at the far end of the yard. She inhaled the soft air, savoring the moment. If she didn't have that damned confession hanging over her head, this would be a perfect morning.

The telephone rang, jolting him awake. It took a moment for Derek to realize he was in bed alone. He stared groggily at the offending instrument before snatching up the receiver.

"Yeah?"

"Oliver Wheatley here, mate."

"Oh, Oliver, hi... Good morning... It is morning, isn't it?"

"I've rung up a wee early, haven't I?" he said with a laugh. "Sorry."

"It's all right. I had a long night that didn't include much sleep," Derek said.

"Lucky you. Well, sorry to wake you, but I shan't take all the blame for disturbing you so early," Oliver said. "Actually, I'm ringing you up at Miranda Maxwell's request.

"You're kidding?"

"Not at all. She arrived early this morning from London. My sodding three-pic package is in trouble and the love was good enough to fly in to help me sort things out. Anyway, we've been chatting over our cornflakes, as it were, and Miranda was most interested to hear she'd negotiated a deal with you over the past few days."

"I can imagine she was."

"In a word, Miranda's distraught about everything that's happened and she wants to set things right. I tried to tell her the problem's not urgent, but she's determined, old man."

"Gee, Oliver, I appreciate her concern, but you're right, there's no particular rush."

Derek sat on the edge of the bed, pulling his thoughts together. As he listened to Oliver he glanced out the window and saw Britt out by the pool, the morning sun gleaming in her blond hair. He was struck by the image, and also relieved to know she hadn't gotten up early and sneaked off.

"Miranda's here at my side now," Oliver said. "Will you chat with her, or shall I have her ring you up later?"

Derek was getting an idea. "Oliver, is there any chance the two of you could come to my place right away? Now that I think about it, there may be something that Miranda could do."

"She'd be delighted, I'm sure. We aren't more than fifteen minutes from there."

"Good. Come on over, then. Tell Miranda I'd like to teach our Miss Kingsley a lesson. Maybe have a little fun of our own while we're at it. After the merry chase she's led us on, she deserves to be the victim of a prank herself."

Oliver chuckled. "Knowing Miranda, it won't take any convincing."

Derek hung up, then glanced out at Britt once more. He rubbed his hands together, anticipating their meeting. Payback time was almost at hand, and he intended to enjoy every blessed moment of it.

It was fifteen minutes after the phone had rung before Derek showed up at the door of the patio. Britt watched him approach. He was wearing jeans and a white cotton turtleneck and he looked absolutely delicious. As he made his way around the pool, bits and snatches of the previous evening filtered through her mind. What agony it was to jeopardize the memory of that! How would she ever be to able to endure it if he wound up hating her for her deceit?

"Up with the birds, I see," Derek said, arriving at the umbrella table.

"Early bird gets the juice," she replied, pointing to her empty glass.

Derek leaned down and kissed her neck, nuzzling her. He smelled wonderful, sending twinges through her as she recalled the feel of his naked body against hers.

"Glad you didn't sneak off without saying goodbye," he said.

"Why would I do that?"

"I don't know. You're full of surprises, Allison. For an innocent, you can be fairly unpredictable." He picked up her empty juice glass. "How about some more?"

Before she could answer, they heard the sound of a doorbell ringing through the open sliding-glass door.

"I wonder who that could be. Excuse me, I'll be back in a sec." He headed for the house. "How about a pastry with some more juice?" he called over his shoulder.

"No, thanks."

As Derek went back inside the house, Britt glanced down at the contract. It was too bad they'd been interrupted before she could get to what she wanted to say. Now she'd have to screw up her courage all over again. She sighed.

Several minutes passed. She began wondering what was going on. What kind of caller would be dropping by this early?

Just then someone came out of the house, but it wasn't Derek. It was Oliver Wheatley and he was carrying a glass of juice. Britt nearly jumped to her feet at the sight of him. What was *he* doing here?

Oliver lumbered toward her, squinting in the bright morning sunlight. As he came around the pool, he saw her plainly. A shocked expression crossed his face.

"Britt? Britt Kingsley, isn't it? From Miranda's office. What on earth are *you* doing here?" Oliver was several feet away. He stopped and gazed around the yard. "I was given to understand Miss O'Donnell was out here, Derek's new screenwriter."

Britt slumped in her chair and groaned. Why didn't the earth just open up and swallow her? It would have been so much kinder.

Oliver continued on, looking very perplexed. "I would have sworn Derek said it was his young lady out here, the lass who did the screenplay." He put the glass of juice down in front of her and scratched his head.

"I'm afraid there's been some confusion, Mr. Wheatley," she said lamely.

"I should think so...." His words trailed off as Derek came out of the house. He was carrying a tray of pastries, a pitcher of juice and a couple of empty glasses. "Ah, here's the man who can clear up the mystery," Oliver said, as Derek approached the table.

Britt closed her eyes, certain at that moment that she'd be better off dead.

"I hope you two managed to introduce yourselves," Derek began cheerfully, setting the tray on the table. "I apologize for not being here, Allison, but one of the great directors of our time hardly needs an introduction." He slapped Oliver on the back. "And Oliver, mark my words, the name Allison O'Donnell will soon be in lights along with the other great writing talents of Hollywood."

Britt put her face into her hand.

"Derek," Oliver said, "we have a wee problem."

"What sort of a problem?"

"I believe you're under a misapprehension, old bean."

Britt looked up at Derek, her face the model of misery. He seemed thoroughly perplexed. He turned to Oliver, then back to her.

"What are you talking about?" Derek asked.

Britt and Oliver exchanged looks.

"I defer to you, my dear," Oliver said.

"Derek," Britt faltered, her voice so shaky she could barely speak, "I'm afraid I've done something absolutely unforgivable." She picked up the contract. "I intended to tell you first thing this morning, but—"

"Tell me what?"

She agonized. "First, let me say that last night—wanting to be with you—was real. There wasn't a thing phony about it." She glanced at Oliver, embarrassed to have him listening to this, but she had to go on. "If you believe nothing else, please believe that."

"Allison, what are you talking about? Why is this sounding like a funeral oration?"

Britt glanced at Oliver, who was sitting there silently. He seemed oddly bemused. She turned back to Derek, who was waiting for her to explain. She opened her mouth to say how sorry she was that she'd lied, how much she regretted it, but it was hard to speak.

"This is awfully embarrassing," she said finally. "Especially considering Mr. Wheatley knows who I really am. The fact is, I've lied to you, Derek. I'm not the person I said I was. I'm a phony. A fraud."

She slid the contract across the table. Derek picked it up. She watched him read it. When he got to the bottom, where she'd signed her name, he glanced up at her. Britt's heart rocked.

"The signature says Britt Kingsley," he said.

She watched his face, hoping to get a hint of what he was thinking. But she couldn't tell a thing. "That's my real name. Allison O'Donnell is a friend of mine. I borrowed her name to hide my true identity because, as Mr. Wheatley here already knows, I work at C.A., as Miranda's assistant."

Derek turned to Oliver, who nodded.

"You can't imagine how shocked I was to come out here and find Miss Kingsley sitting by your pool, old bean."

"I had to use a pseudonym," Britt explained, "because when you called the office that first time, asking for Miranda, I told you my name was Britt...and you made a little joke about it, Derek. Remember?"

He nodded, putting down the contract. "Yes. But that was no reason to put another name on your screenplay. Unless you're saying you didn't write *Dream Girl.*"

"Oh, I wrote it, all right. That's the problem. C.A. doesn't allow self-dealing. That's a big rule. I took my job there under false pretenses. It was wrong, but I was desperate. I knew I could write, but I couldn't get anyone to read my work. I even sent you something once but you sent it back unread.

"So I got the idea that if I worked at C.A. I might make some contacts, have a chance to tell someone about my work. You were my first opportunity. When you called, saying you were in the market for a project, it was like a dream come true."

"And when I showed interest in the script, you sent it off under another name. Allison O'Donnell."

She nodded, biting her lip.

"And I bought it—hook, line and sinker." He glanced over at Oliver, shaking his head. "I guess there's a sucker born every minute."

"If you say so, old man. But I wouldn't be too hard on myself, if I were you. Our Miss Kingsley is a clever girl."

"I really didn't mean to hurt anyone," Britt pleaded. "I had no idea things would get so complicated. In fact, I was hoping it could all be done by mail."

Derek and Oliver exchanged long looks.

"This ever happen to you, Oliver?" Derek asked.

"Can't say that it has, old man."

Derek shook his head. "I'm not quite sure what a guy's supposed to do in a situation like this. It's sort of the equivalent of being seduced under false pretense."

"Rather dicey, all right," Oliver agreed.

"They'll be joking about this at the Polo Lounge for years," Derek said woefully.

Britt knew she was being the made the butt of their black humor, but she was hardly in a position to complain. "You have every right to hate me, Derek. I can't blame you. My mistake was wanting to sell my screen-play too badly. I realize now that what you think of me is much more important than making a sale. So I'm going to make it easy for you."

She reached across the table, picked up the contract, and tore it in half, then tore it in half again.

Derek watched her, surprise on his face. "Why did you do that?"

"Because honesty, integrity, and my own self-respect demand it."

Derek and Oliver looked at each other again.

"The lady understands drama," Oliver declared. "That much is real."

"No, this is her and she's speaking from the heart. I can tell," Derek said.

Britt eyes filled. "Thank you."

Derek reached over and patted her hand.

Just then, she saw movement out of the corner of her eye. The iron gate at the side yard opened and a woman came though it. When Britt saw that it was Miranda Maxwell, she just about died all over again.

"Well, here you are!" Miranda called as the men turned. "I've been ringing the bloody chimes for five minutes."

Derek and Oliver got to their feet. Britt sat frozen like the proverbial deer caught in the headlights of a car.

"Jolly glad to see you made it, Miranda," Oliver called to her.

"Miranda?" Derek said.

"Oh, Lord," Britt muttered. She scrunched down in her chair, wishing she'd never been born.

"I had a call from her this morning, shortly before heading this way," Oliver explained. "She's just in from London to help me sort out my bloody three-pic package that's gone awry. I told her to pop by and join us. Hope you don't mind, old man."

Britt groaned the groan of the dying as Miranda, in a crisp blue suit and Liberty scarf, approached them. She couldn't bear to watch. She buried her face in her hands.

"This is not Miranda Maxwell," she heard Derek mumble to Oliver.

"What's that, mate?"

"Hello and good morning!" Miranda said cheerily. She gave Oliver a kiss. "And you, dear boy, must be the illustrious Derek Redmond!" she added, turning to Derek. "I'm so terribly pleased to meet you!"

They shook hands. Derek appeared to be stunned.

"I say," Miranda said, leaning around him, "is that you, Britt? What in heaven's name are you doing here?"

"Odd," Oliver said. "I asked the same question."

Miranda regarded them all quizzically.

"You are not the woman I had a drink with last night at Musso & Frank Grill," Derek announced.

Miranda blinked. "I should hope not, love. I spent the night in an airplane flying in from London."

"We seem to have another mystery on our hands," Oliver observed, rubbing his hands together with glee.

Derek grabbed a chair for Miranda and they all sat down. Britt couldn't have felt any worse if she were

Marie Antoinette on her way to the guillotine. In fact, it might have been better.

"Would somebody care to explain the mystery bit?" Miranda requested airily.

There was a brief silence, then Derek spoke. "For the past several days you and I have been negotiating an option agreement for Allison O'Donnell's screenplay."

"How terribly fascinating," Miranda replied. "I do hope I squeezed every penny out of you I could. By the way, who's Allison O'Donnell?"

Derek and Oliver looked at each other. Britt closed her eyes.

"Your assistant, Miranda."

"My assistant, you say? Allison O'Donnell? Heavens, I do seem to have developed a mild case of amnesia, don't I?"

Britt couldn't bear it anymore. All her chickens were coming home to roost at once. "What they're trying to say, Miranda, is that I've deceived you as well as Derek."

Her eyes widened. "Pray, do go on."

"I assumed the name Allison O'Donnell to sell my screenplay to Derek."

"*Your* screenplay?"

"Yes. I used your office and name to promote my interests while you were in England. It was very foolish. I've already tried to apologize to Derek for the embarrassment I've caused him. I owe you an apology, as well. I meant no harm, but I screwed up badly just the same."

Miranda seemed stunned. She blinked, opened her mouth to speak, shut it, then finally said, "Quite a homecoming, I must say."

"You warned me about self-dealing," Britt went on, "but in your absence, I promoted myself anyway. I have no choice but to resign, I know. I've breached your trust and I'm very sorry for any embarrassment I've caused you."

"I appreciate that, Britt. It isn't the first time I've been taken advantage of and, I dare say, it won't be the last. But it doesn't explain how I managed to have a drink with Mr. Redmond last evening while to the best of my knowledge I was somewhere over the North Pole about then."

"I've been curious about that, myself," Derek said.

The three of them—Derek, Miranda and Oliver—all turned to her.

Britt's insides turned to Jell-O. She swallowed hard. They waited. She summoned her courage for the final mea culpa. "Bloody hell," she said in her best Miranda accent, "I'd rather die than admit this, especially with Miranda sitting here, but the awful truth is, you're looking at her, ducks."

There was a brief silence. Then Miranda began laughing hysterically. Oliver joined her. They were soon red in the face. Derek was incredulous.

"You mean . . . you . . ."

Britt nodded.

"I've been in Hollywood for three years now," Miranda said, "but this is the dottiest charade I've yet to encounter. Good Lord, Britt, you're priceless!"

She went off again into gales of laughter. Oliver wiped his eyes.

But Derek was just shaking his head. "But how...did you manage to..."

"The real Allison O'Donnell helped me pull it off," Britt explained. "She knows a makeup artist at Paramount who has the ability to completely transform people. I know it was crazy of me to do it, Derek, but I was desperate."

He could hardly speak. "That woman last night at Musso & Frank...was really *you?*"

"Yes, and it was me you spoke with on the phone all those times."

"But what about that call at the Polo Lounge? *I* phoned her."

"No, you called the office and *she* called you back." Britt chewed on her lip. "That was me—calling from a pay phone by the rest rooms."

Miranda and Oliver both dabbed their eyes as they listened. Miranda touched Derek's arm. "Darling, if you don't have the rights to this story, you must get them immediately."

Derek shook his head, a reluctant smile filling his face. "This is unbelievable. I had a drink with this woman and hadn't the slightest idea."

"I'm not proud of it," Britt said. "I didn't even want to do it. But I kept getting sucked in deeper and deeper. All I wanted was for you to read my screenplay and like it."

"You certainly accomplished that."

She searched his eyes. "Do you hate me?" she asked. "Or are you just disgusted?"

He drew a long breath. "I'm more shocked than anything."

"I know what I did was wrong, but I didn't mean to harm either of you," she added, glancing Miranda's way. "I just wanted you to love *Dream Girl*, Derek."

"Lord," Miranda said as she looked back and forth between them. "I don't know whether to laugh again or cry. Perhaps you can help, Derek. Is this the moment for us to tearfully embrace? Or do we ring up our solicitors?"

"I'm not into guilt and blame, Miranda."

"You're suggesting we should let her off the hook? No hanging her by her thumbs or fifty lashes with a cat-o'-nine-tails?"

"The issue, the only issue as far as I'm concerned," Derek said, "is whether I get that script."

"I thought I—that is, my alter ego—already negotiated an option agreement with you for the screenplay."

Derek picked up the torn pieces of the option form and arranged them in front of Miranda. "Miss Kingsley has opted to rescind the contract."

"Oh, dear. You mean I haven't earned a commission, after all?"

Miranda and Oliver chuckled.

"I consider this an urgent matter," Derek said. "You're her agent, Miranda. What are we going to do?"

Miranda looked Britt in the eye. "All joking aside, you did intend that I represent you."

"Well . . . I . . ."

"We can draw up the agency agreement later, dear. A verbal arrangement will do for now." Miranda studied the form arrayed before her. "With all due respect, Britt, in future you should keep to your writing and leave the agenting to me."

"Is there something wrong?" Derek asked.

"You took advantage of the girl." She paused, and looked up at Britt. "Not that she didn't deserve it, mind you. But I'd never let a client of mine sign anything like this. You do like the script, don't you?"

"It's potential Oscar material."

"In that case, I'd say we start negotiations at triple the figure you've listed here."

"What?"

"You want the project, don't you?"

"I thought we already had a deal," he protested.

"It was negotiated under false pretenses. I'm afraid you're dealing with me now, darling. You'll have to do better if you want this script."

Derek glanced at Britt. "I never should have let you tear that up."

Britt didn't know if they were putting her on—getting their pound of flesh—or if it was for real. "This is a joke, right? You're just getting even with me?"

"I can't force you to accept me as your agent," Miranda answered blandly, "but I do hate to see you being taken advantage of. We can do better than this, assuming they're right about the caliber of your work. And if Derek won't talk turkey, as you Yanks say, then we'll have to look elsewhere."

"Hey," Derek protested, "I'm the innocent victim here."

"Not so innocent as you'd have us believe," Miranda replied. "Fun's fun, but it's time to get down to business. You've heard our price, love. Do you want Britt's screenplay, or not?"

"All right, it's a deal."

"And twenty-five for option money is far too little," Miranda declared. "We want fifty and not a penny less."

He grimaced. "I think I liked the other Miranda better."

Miranda regaled him with bemused laughter, then checked her watch. "Heavens, we're late, Oliver. We must tend to your problem."

She rose, as did Oliver.

"Derek, I'll have a new agreement drawn up and delivered to you by this afternoon. We must be on our way now, however. The time's gotten on."

Oliver, who'd been taking it all in with a look of utter fascination, said, "This has been delightfully zany, I must say—more amusing, even, than a few of the pictures I've made. I'd almost rather stay."

"Sorry, Oliver. I think our friends would rather be alone," Miranda said. "Am I right, Derek?"

"It might not be a bad idea if you did leave," he replied, "while I've still got a shirt on my back."

"Oh, nonsense." Miranda took Oliver's arm. "You've enjoyed every minute of this." She glanced at Britt. "It might be a good idea if you come by the office and clean out your desk, love. I'll have a client agreement ready for you to sign. I'm not cheap, but you'll end up making more with me handling your affairs—and you staying out of mine.''

''I don't remember ever being screwed and enjoying it so much,'' Derek muttered dryly.

''Britt,'' Miranda said, ''when we've gone, do console the man.'' She led Oliver toward the house. ''Come along, dear, let's get your deal back on track so I can get on a bloody plane back to England.''

Oliver gave Britt and Derek a wink. ''I love this town. If it didn't exist, somebody would have to invent it.''

Britt and Derek stared at each other for a long time after Miranda and Oliver left.

''Come on, love,'' he said, pulling her to her feet, ''let's go inside and have some breakfast.''

Britt stopped him, holding both his hands. ''Do you really forgive me? You don't hate me for what I did?''

''Oh, don't worry, I'm going to rub your nose in it every once in a while. But no, I don't hate you. Truth be known, I think I've fallen in love with you.''

''Really?'' She looked into his eyes.

''Yes.''

''I love you, too.''

He gave her a penetrating look. ''I can trust that?''

''Oh, definitely. I'll never lie to you again, Derek. I promise. I've learned my lesson. I truly have.''

He folded her arm over his and started toward the house. Britt stopped him.

"Wait! I have to know. Did all that last bit at the end really happen? Are you going to buy my screenplay? It's not a hoax, is it? Revenge for what I did?"

He grinned. "Hell, no. I kid about a lot of things, Britt, but money isn't one of them. Do you have any idea what *Dream Girl* will cost me now? Miranda just made you a very wealthy woman—at *my* expense."

She put her arms around his waist. "Aren't I worth it?"

He held her face in his hands, then leaned over and kissed her lightly on the lips. "I guess we'll have to wait and see."

"You mean until the box-office receipts come in?"

He nodded.

"What if it flops?"

"Then let's hope we've had a hell of a lot of fun getting from here to there."

He kissed her again. They smiled into each other's eyes.

"Something else just occurred to me," he said.

"What's that?"

"You're unemployed. You told Miranda you'd resign and she told you to clean out your desk."

"So?"

"So, you don't have anything to do today—except drop by C.A. later to sign your agreement."

"So?"

"So you might as well spend the rest of the morning here with me."

"Doing what?" she asked.

"I thought maybe we could research some love scenes."

Britt gave him a look. "Which love scenes are we talking about, Mr. Redmond? Mine? Or the ones in my screenplay?"

Derek grinned at her. "Funny how the lines between fact and fiction get blurred, isn't it?"

"Are you going to tease me forever for what I did?" she asked.

He gathered her close. "I guess not. It would hardly be fair, considering . . ."

Britt pulled away a bit and looked him straight in the eye. "Considering what?"

"That I knew you were a fake almost from the beginning."

She blanched. "No. You didn't. You're just saying that to make me suffer a little more."

Derek shook his head. "No. After we spoke the first time, I had lunch with Oliver and he happened to mention that Miranda was in England. When I didn't believe him, he even called her there to prove it to me. I spoke with her housekeeper."

Britt was dumbfounded. "Then you knew all along?"

"I knew Miranda was fake. I figured you were, too, until we talked about the script. I didn't discover that you were Britt Kingsley until I drove Oliver to C.A. and we saw you come out of the building. I knew you as Allison, and Oliver pointed you out as Miranda's assistant."

"You mean Oliver and Miranda were in on everything that just happened? The three of you put on that little drama to embarrass and humiliate me?"

"No, it was actually to teach you a lesson."

"Teach me a lesson!"

He gave her a look. "You aren't suggesting you didn't deserve it?"

She lowered her eyes. "No, you're right, I did."

"I'll tell you this, Britt. Nobody will ever match your performance of the past few days. I'd never have guessed that the woman at Musso & Frank Grill was the one I slept with last night." He playfully cuffed her chin. "Perhaps you ought to revive your acting career, my love. You might have missed a bet."

She shook her head. "No, thanks. I never want to be anyone but myself again. No more acting and no more lies. I've reformed."

Derek gave her another long, lingering kiss. When the caress ended, he pulled back, looked into her eyes, and said, "That's fine by me, because the woman I made love with last night is the one I want."

"It was me, Derek. Honest."

"Never change," he said, holding her. "Because I love you just the way you are."

* * * * *

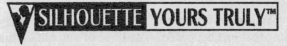

Sneak Previews of February titles, from Yours Truly

The 7lb., 2 oz. Valentine—Marie Ferrarella
Book 3 of Marie's The Baby of the Month Club cross-line miniseries!

Erin Collins is a mom-to-be, but the dad-to-be is nowhere to be found. So she places a personal ad, desperately seeking her baby's daddy, and Brady Lockwood finally turns up. But he has no idea who Erin is—or why she'd be handing him a cigar!

How Much Is that Couple in the Window? —Lori Herter
Book 1 of Lori's Million-Dollar Marriages miniseries

Salesclerk Jennifer Westgate's new job is to live in a department store window for a week as the new bride of a gorgeous groom. The sidewalk shoppers love them, the window gets steamier every night, but her make-believe husband is hardly a happy newlywed!

Are your lips succulent, impetuous, delicious or racy?

Find out in a very special Valentine's Day promotion—THAT SPECIAL KISS!

Inside four special Harlequin and Silhouette February books are details for THAT SPECIAL KISS! explaining how you can have your lip prints read by a romance expert.

Look for details in the following series books, written by four of Harlequin and Silhouette readers' favorite authors:

Silhouette Intimate Moments #691
Mackenzie's Pleasure by *New York Times* bestselling author Linda Howard

Harlequin Romance #3395
Because of the Baby by Debbie Macomber

Silhouette Desire #979
Megan's Marriage by Annette Broadrick

Harlequin Presents #1793
The One and Only by Carole Mortimer

Fun, romance, four top-selling authors, plus a **FREE** gift! This is a very special Valentine's Day you won't want to miss! Only from Harlequin and Silhouette.

VAL96

HOW MUCH IS THAT
COUPLE IN THE WINDOW?
by Lori Herter

Book 1 of Lori's Million-Dollar
Marriages miniseries
Yours Truly™—February

Salesclerk Jennifer Westgate's new job is to live in a
department store display window for a week as the
bride of a gorgeous groom. Here's what sidewalk
shoppers have to say about them:

*"Why is the window so steamy tonight? I can't see what
they're doing!"* —Henrietta, age 82

*"That mousey bride is hardly Charles Derring's type. It's
me who should be living in the window with him!"*
—Delphine, Charles's soon-to-be ex-girlfriend

*"Jennifer never modeled pink silk teddies for me! This is
an outrage!"*
—Peter, Jennifer's soon-to-be ex-boyfriend

"How much is that couple in the window?"
—Timmy, age 9

HOW MUCH IS THAT COUPLE IN THE WINDOW?
by Lori Herter—Book 1 of her Million-Dollar Marriages
miniseries—available in February from

▼ SILHOUETTE YOURS TRULY™

Love—when you least expect it!

It's our 1000th Special Edition and we're celebrating!

Join us these coming months for some wonderful stories in a special celebration of our 1000th book with some of your favorite authors!

Diana Palmer　　　　**Nora Roberts**
Debbie Macomber　　**Christine Flynn**
Phyllis Halldorson　　**Lisa Jackson**

Plus miniseries by:

Lindsay McKenna, Marie Ferrarella, Sherryl Woods and Gina Ferris Wilkins.

And many more books by special writers!

And as a special bonus, all Silhouette Special Edition titles published during Celebration 1000! will have **_double_** Pages & Privileges proofs of purchase!

Silhouette Special Edition...heartwarming stories packed with emotion, just for you! You'll fall in love with our next 1000 special stories!

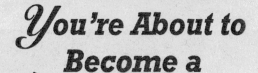

You're About to Become a

Privileged Woman

Reap the rewards of fabulous free gifts and benefits with proofs-of-purchase from Silhouette and Harlequin books

Pages & Privileges™

It's our way of thanking you for buying our books at your favorite retail stores.

✂

```
┌─────────────────────────┐
│  PROOF OF    YT-PP99     │
│  PURCHASE                │
│ Offer expires October 31, 1996 │
└─────────────────────────┘
```

**Harlequin and Silhouette—
the most privileged readers in the world!**

For more information about Harlequin and Silhouette's PAGES & PRIVILEGES program call the Pages & Privileges Benefits Desk: 1-503-794-2499

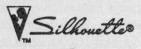

YT-PP99